Write Now!

EXPRESSIONS OF YOUTH

Edited by Chris Hallam

First published in Great Britain in 2003 by
YOUNG WRITERS
Remus House,
Coltsfoot Drive,
Peterborough, PE2 9JX
Telephone (01733) 890066

All Rights Reserved

Copyright Contributors 2003

SB ISBN 1 84460 258 3

FOREWORD

This year, Young Writers proudly presents a showcase of the best short stories and creative writing from today's up-and-coming writers.

We set the challenge of writing for one of our four themes - 'Myths & Legends', 'Hold The Front Page', 'A Day In The Life Of . . .' and 'Short Stories/Fiction'. The effort and imagination expressed by each individual writer was more than impressive and made selecting entries an enjoyable, yet demanding, task.

Write Now! Expressions Of Youth is a collection that we feel you are sure to enjoy - featuring the very best young authors of the future. Their hard work and enthusiasm clearly shines within these pages, highlighting the achievement each piece represents.

We hope you are as pleased with the final selection as we are and that you will continue to enjoy this special collection for many years to come.

Contents

Jessica Bagust	1
Leeann Rowan	2
Danielle Leman	3
Oliver Astington	4
Rebecca Smith	6

Aith Junior High School, Shetland

Debbie Wynn	7
Lauren Bulter	12
Anna Mackenzie	14
Gary Lockyer	15
Lewis Garrick	16
Fiona Morrison	17
Darren Hodge	18
Aimee Keith	20
Lauren Walterson	22
Kristian Fraser	23
Inga Tulloch	24

Ash Green School, West Midlands

Megan Hyde & Zoe Green	25
Chanice Relton	26
Kyrie Gallagher	27
Jamie Brassington	28
Emma Moore	29
Samantha Sanders	30
Ben Morris	31
Adam Durran	32

Islamia Girls' School, London

Hafsah Ahmed	33

Joseph Leckie Community School, West Midlands

Tanya Collier	35
Katharine Morgan	36
Sarah Ashcroft	37

Symran Khangura	38
Aaisha Sidat & Aysha Sidat	39

Langdon School, London

Matthew A Hector	40
Sohail Mohammed	42
Christopher Worby	43
Adil Rahman	44
Mohammed Akram	45
Samba Kabwe	46
Ikram Samater	48
Samina Karim	49
Khalid Jeeva	50
Sam Gray	51
Vijay Davdra	52
Habezur Rahman	53
Mariya Rashid	54
Amarpreet Kaur	55
Mandip Singh	56
Christine Rodrigues	58
Jahad Uddin	59
Vibenche Yasocumaran	60
Elakkiya Sunthararajan	61
Jessica Manning	62
Cinduja Surendran	64
Priya Shah	65
Khris Johal	66
Rajah Safrat	67
Aswathi Nair	68
Dulal Rahman	70
Jeevan Jyothyprakash	71
Raeesa Kaiser	72
Gurminderjit Boparai	73
Muneer Patel	74
Jasmin Bansal	76
Jermaine Anderson	77
Janki Vaghela	78
Ashley Davis	80

Wasif Saeed Sheikh	82
May Sulaiman	84
Aliya Malik	85

Les Beaucamps Secondary School, Guernsey
Catie Le Prevost	86

Ludlow CE School, Shropshire
Thomas Lynam	87

Parklands High School, Manchester
Melissa Koekemoer	88
Kelsey Easton	89
Aviva Nelson	90
Jessica Gibson	92
Lacey Holden	93
Emma McMenamin	94
Scott Wilkinson	95
Shauna Summers	96
Andrew Taylor	97
Alex Hickson	98
Rachel Porritt	99

Pierowall Junior High School, Orkney
Kirsty Cable	100

Pool Hayes Community School, West Midlands
Amy Yates	102
Steven Morris	104
Sarah Whitehouse	105
Greg Corbett	106
Alex Faulkner	107
Jessie Edwards	108
Cally Staffiere	109
Donna Russon	110
Toni-Anne Ashcroft	111

Ramsey Grammar School, Isle Of Man

Rebecca Vaughan	112
Sian Howes	113
Katie Jones	114
Shelley Harper	115
Graeme Osborn	116
Adam Millard	117
Terry Ayres	118
Samantha Westcott	119
Kimberley Counsell	120
Christopher Smith	121
David Hicks	122
Daniel Oram	123

St Anne's School, Alderney

Vikki Knight	124
Lianne Bunn	125
Ellie Gaudion	126
Iain Macfarlane	127
Lauren Jean	128
Jennifer Bohan	129
Stephen Blondin	130
Bonnie Flewitt	131
Kirsty Walters	132
Liam Sumner	134
Rhys Jenkins	135
Nicola Crawford	136
Ryan Murray	138
Gemma Johns	139
Adele Woodruff	140
Samantha Gaudion	141
Joseph Gaudion	142
Hannah Llewellyn	143
Matthew Collins	144
David Chadney	145
David Jennings	146
Matthew Smith	147

St Edmund's Catholic School, West Midlands
        Ryan Blaney 148
        Angelo Franco 149
        Jennifer Galloway 150
        Cameron Chumber 151
        Ruth Ewins 152

St Francis Of Assisi RC School, West Midlands
        Anthony Cooke 153
        Helen Keenan 154
        David Shaw 155

Sanday Junior High School, Orkney
        Chris Masters 156
        Andrew Walls 158
        Luke Smith 159

Sgoil Nan Loch, Isle Of Lewis
        Dawn Mackenzie 160
        Sean Mills 161
        Elizabeth Macleod 162
        Penny Curry 163
        John Macdonald 164
        Fiona Mackenzie 165
        Alexander Mackenzie 166
        Jacqueline Laing 167
        Anne Macleod 168
        Karen Mackay 169
        David Robertson 170
        Ruth Sara Mason 171
        Duncan Macrae 172
        Karen Mackenzie 173
        Jane Macleod 174

The Priory School, Shropshire
        Adelaide Stokes 175
        Lauren Walker 176
        Laura Veecock 177

Helen Alexander	178
Holly Edwards	179
Caroline James	180
Siobhan Hinton	181
Mia Tivey	182
Eloise Jackson	184
Rachel Benson	185

The Streetly School, West Midlands
Lisa Patel	186

Wakefield Girls' High School, West Yorkshire
Harriet Aldam	188
Lucy Alliott	190
Alice Castle	192
Samantha Antwis	194
Jessica Barrell	195
Joanne Morris	196
Helen Palfrey	198
Kate Elizabeth Hulley	200
Reena Patel	201
Vicky Peacock	202
Ileena Pramanik	203
Sarah Smith	204
Danielle Saunders	206

Ysgol Uwchradd Tregaron, Ceredigion
Beth Langley	207
Rachel Burrowes	208

The Creative Writing

TOP SPEED

Now as she walked down the road to the shops, Elle pulled her scarf tightly around her face to conceal from those around her, the tears now steadily rolling down her cheeks. The passing friendly faces that waved to her only received in return a small nod or grunt, if lucky. They all seemed to have forgotten about her loss, she still felt it was yesterday, although it was much longer ago. The tears now tumbled down her face and she could feel herself about to lose control, she could remember the crash clearly.

Elle had been stood outside her house when her mother had rushed down the hill. Her mother was running to a dog that was lying in the middle of the road, having been hit by a passing car; Elle's mother had always been an animal lover. The car which was driving well over the speed limit had not stopped and nor had any of the other traffic. As her mother reached parallel with the animal, Elle began to run down to her mother, curious as to what was going on. It was too late, a car came over the hill at top speed and as it had no time to stop, swerved to dodge the car that had stopped to help Elle's mother and instead, hit her.

As Elle reached the shop entrance, another figure began to wave frantically, this was one of her many friends, Katie. At least she had them. Her friend rushed over, so she quickly put on a brave face.
'How are you?' her friend asked, as happily as ever.
'OK!' Elle replied strongly.

Jessica Bagust (13)

STRANGER

Another day in Clevemore High School. It seemed a mundane experience to some, but to one special boy it was a new, exciting adventure.

'I'd like to introduce you to a new pupil - Robert James.'
Next to the small, round, bald headteacher was a tall, good-looking boy with golden-brown hair and glowing blue eyes. Whispers filled the room, soon erupting into a conversation with the 'new boy'. He suddenly became popular. Everyone was intrigued by his stories of being a superb sports star and athlete at his old school, travelling from village to city in his 14 years.

During lunch there was a large crowd surrounding Robert, all asking him about his life and what he got up to. He enjoyed the attention all day and made so many new friends. No one ignored him. He was so happy with the reaction he got, he decided to show his true self.

He stepped into the classroom, waiting for a response. Silence filled the room. Suddenly a burst of laughter broke the silence. His exterior changed to slimy blue flesh with random purple patterns. Three tentacles stretched from his large forehead. Despite being unable to bleed or breathe like his classmates, he could still cry like them. He cried at the hypocritical attitude of his classmates.

He was a superb sports star at his old school and he did travel a lot. He did do all the things he told his classmates. Of course they were all performed in foreign ways, but he was still the same being. Why did they reject him?

Leeann Rowan (14)

A DAY IN THE LIFE OF MARY CLARK

This true story is about my great grandma and it's about her nightmare and ours. She is 87 years old and she can hardly walk with her small, wide walking stick. She just manages to stroll along.

The story begins with my great grandma and great grandad going to bed. They fell asleep quite quickly because they were very tired, but in the middle of the night they both woke up. They both stumbled into the room and great grandad sat in his favourite chair. He asked for a cup of water as he was feeling a bit dizzy. Grandma went to get him one. Bringing the ice-cold drink in she dropped it. She was shaking, because great grandad wasn't moving. He was sat quite still. Walking over to him she said his name, but there was nothing, not even an answer. She got closer and nudged him, but nothing. She called the ambulance, thinking there wasn't anything else she could do. The ambulance and the paramedics told her that he had had a heart attack. She started to cry with shock.

In the morning everyone was sad. My mum had been crying all day and I had been crying as well. Mum got told first on the phone. I found out when Mum told Dad because I wouldn't move from behind the door and because Mum was crying. I burst out crying when I found out as well. It was very sad for us all. We often go and visit his grave. We all miss him.

Danielle Leman

BELGIUM 1914

Under the sticky, shimmering heat of the August sun, the tired troopers waited in the deserted farmhouse near Mons. A young lieutenant, Sebastian Fletcher of the 16th Lancers, took the brief respite from the retreat to wet his dry, cracked gullet. *Like the road,* he thought, looking towards the horizon.

There was a fatalistic air around the place and he wiped his grimy brow with a sweating, slippery hand. His horse stood idly by, lapping up some water from a bucket. His men sat inside the whitewashed building, playing cards and grumbling. As his attentions turned westwards, he noticed a smouldering pyre of dust being kicked up. He wondered what the lone rider wanted. *God, give me some peace,* thought Sebastian.

A few minutes later, the brown horse and its rider swerved into the farmyard. The man flung himself from the saddle. The young lieutenant walked over to him and noting the insignia on the man's epaulettes, took him to be a full captain from HQ.
'I'm Captain Henry Knowles . . . general headquarters . . . and you are?' panted the officer.
'Lieutenant Fletcher, Sir, 16th Lancers,' replied Sebastian.
'You're commanding this company, Lieutenant?' asked his superior, surprised.
'Yes Sir. The captain was killed yesterday in a skirmish. Major's missing.' His company was in a sorry state.
'You're to lead a counter attack . . .'

It was a quarter of an hour since his men had saddled up. Bamboo lances in holsters and swords jangling from their belts, they neared the supposed site of the German encampment. Calling his anxious men to a halt, he scanned the horizon, shielding his eyes from the sun with a hand. Amongst some spindly trees, he spotted the blurred outline of a sentry. They cantered forwards, his men grinning. He had no doubt of their courage.

At 300 yards he ordered the charge. Lances levelled, they propelled themselves towards the enemy, horses panting, hooves pounding, kicking up dust and mud.

The German on guard was not concentrating on his task. As the fifty khaki-clad lancers of C Company cascaded towards him, he could only gasp and croak a warning to his comrades who sat at the edge of the field, drinking and laughing.

Sebastian was at the front and was first to burst into the midst of the Germans. Startled, they fumbled for the bolts on their rifles - no use. The lancers hit home, the finest cavalry the world possessed. The brass-spike helmeted Bavarians broke in terror into the adjacent field, towards a hedgerow.

Not realising any danger, he led his men onwards, pursuing the routing men who threw away packs and shovels to save themselves. Many had lost their headgear and screamed as they were impaled on lance tips. Under the blue sky, where hawks hovered, the hunters chased the running foe like foxes.

Suddenly, Sebastian glanced a dull black shape in the tree line, too late. A stuttering but resonant stream of bullets smacked home. His men were chopped from their saddles, mounts fell in a sea of flesh and dust. He looked to his right, then fell into the grass amongst the wounded. His vision blurred, he felt for his revolver. A seething horde of grey-clad men ran at him. Blood ran in rivulets down his tunic from the gaping hole in his shoulder.
I'm dead, he thought and all went black . . .

Oliver Astington (15)

LOST IN FRANCE

Help, I'm in France, looking for someone to rescue me. I've been walking around all day and night. All I've had to eat is a fish on a stick that hadn't been cooked properly.

Ashley went to France to stay with her nan. She was due to catch the plane and she got locked in the loo. On her way she met a little fluffy dog and he followed her all day long. Then suddenly the fluffy dog led her to a castle.

Ashley slowly tiptoed to the beautiful golden door with the fluffy dog that she called Fluffy next to her. She anxiously knocked on the door.
'Yes my dear, how can I help you?' said the lady.
'I'm lost,' whispered Ashley.
'OK, you can come in.'
'Thanks,' said Ashley nervously as she went into the castle and sat down at the patterned table. She asked to go into the garden.

Ashley and Fluffy strolled around the wood in the back garden. It was surrounded with flowers of all kinds. Then suddenly a door began to open and there, straight in front of her, was the most beautiful bird Ashley had ever seen in her life. The feathers were so soft, but this bird was not a normal bird. It was the most lovely bird in the world and it was the only one of its kind left. Suddenly the bird asked kindly for Ashley and Fluffy to get on his back, so they did. The bird flew into the night whilst Ashley and Fluffy looked up at the stars. Then the bird dropped them back home safely in England.
'Thank you beautiful bird,' said Ashley.

Rebecca Smith (12)

A DAY IN THE LIFE OF STEVE MCQUINTY

Monday 11th, 5am
Hey there, my name is Steve McQuinty. I'm thirteen and I live in Northumberland (that's in northern England). This is a day in my life! Okay then, right, you know my name, age and where I live, so I suppose I'd better tell you about the day I've had. Well, it started like this . . .

I woke up at three in the morning with my little sister screaming in my ear, saying, 'Lala want wada Teve, peas?' So that meant me having to get up and get her some 'wada'. If only I hadn't offered to look after her for one night, this wouldn't have happened, although on the other hand I'd have then been stuck with a 65-year-old fart and had to go to bed a nine (trust me, this has happened before, several times). Well, no matter which way I went, I'd still have been stuck in the middle of disaster.

I decided to go back to bed when I realised that there was no point because I would only be woken up in three minutes. My little sister, if only I had one shot, one shot, I'd give her a piece of my mind.

Monday 11th, 7am
I was just lying in my bed when all of a sudden I heard the school bus pull up outside. I looked at my watch. It was *seven!* I raced downstairs (not realising that I was still in my pyjamas). I had to run after the bus and when it stopped, the girl I fancied saw me in my Snoopy pyjamas. I felt my face go red. I decided that maybe I wouldn't go to school today because of my embarrassment.

When I went inside the house, I was greeted by the ringing of the phone. I answered it and it was Mum doing her usual check up. This is what she said, 'Hi Steve! Just me saying that, um, hold on a minute! Steve, why aren't you at school?'
'Funny you mentioned that, Mum. You see, I sorta missed the bus. I didn't hear my alarm go off and, and . . . '
'I don't want to hear it, Steve. You've missed too many days. I don't know *what* I'm going to do with you. I'm just so disappointed in you,' she said.

I was so worried about what I would hear next, but I think it wasn't too bad. Maybe it was!

'Sorry. Now how is Laura? More to the point, where is she?'

I think she meant that if I couldn't look after myself, I wouldn't be able to look after my own sister. But then I realised something - where was Laura?

Monday 11th, 1pm

This was the point when I needed somebody to help me calm down. Mum and Dad would be back in three hours and I still had no idea what I was going to do. What would Mum say? How long would she cry for? How long would I be grounded for? Would she care? Would I be disowned? I think the last answer would be *yes*. I wasn't even hungry. I'm always hungry! Perhaps it was the pressure. I think I'm going crazy here. Wait a minute! If I'm so worried, then why wasn't I out looking for her? C'mon Steve, let's go!

I set off on my hunt when I saw the cupboard door open. I peered inside and it was her, the little runt. Ooh! Now she's in trouble!

'Why have you been in there? You know you're not supposed to be in there. You scared the living s**t out of me,' I said quite abruptly.

'Lala sorry, Teve. Me no mean to scare you,' she said, almost too sweetly. And that smile, it was so sweet. I just had to give in to her. Maybe she's not that bad after all.

'Okay, I'll let you off this time, but remember, only once,' I said as if I really meant it. Maybe I should let her off a couple more times - she is only small.

'Now let's get you something to eat. What would you like?' I asked, almost making myself sound queer.

Monday 11th, 3pm

We finished our sarnies at about half one. She kept on saying to me that she would never scare me like that again.

We were watching 'The Little Mermaid Returns To The Ocean' (that being her fave video), when we heard voices outside. They sure were weird. I told Laura to hide, but she just sat there smiling. I asked her why she hadn't moved and she said that she wouldn't because it was probably Mummy and Daddy. I said it wasn't them because it wasn't their voices. Of course, she didn't believe me and ran outside. Then two men came inside, one holding a sack and the other holding *her!* I grasped the kitchen knife and threatened to use it on them. I recognised their faces. It was Bob and Blunder, our next-door neighbours! It was probably them playing a prank, so I told them to put her down and they started laughing. I wondered why?

I said, 'Bob, Blunder, put her down.'

They looked at each other and said, 'Steve, how'd you know it was us?' They sounded pretty surprised. As if they were really trying to rob us!

'Guys, what's the bag for?' I pondered.

They looked at each other and then looked at the bag. They put it behind their backs.

'You see, Steve, we didn't realise you were in and thought that if we tried, we could take back the things you borrowed,' they said, looking quite the fools.

Suddenly, a car pulled up on our drive. As soon as Bob heard the car, he poked Blunder and they ran out before I could ask them where they were going. This car I had never seen before, but whoever it was, they certainly were in a hurry. Somebody got out of the car. They ran inside the house. It sure was amazing how fast this old bird could run! I heard the door slam and guess who it was? My mum, huffing and puffing as if she had just run for Britain.

'Mummy!' shouted Laura. 'Lala missed you so much.'

'Laura, thank goodness you're alright,' Mum said, holding her like she had never held her before. 'Where is your brother?'

'Hey Mum, don't I get a hug?' I asked, expecting her to say okay.

'Why do you think I would give you a hug, *boy?*' She was going to shout, but she said it calmly - aggressively, but calmly.

'Mum, maybe I can explain . . . ' I had barely started when she interrupted.

'Oh really? Explain to me why you weren't at school today? Why did you hang up on me earlier today? C'mon son, you can normally make up stories, so why not today?' She was obviously getting tired of me telling her rubbish. 'Steve, I am really annoyed at you, so don't even bother about being punished. This is because I can't even look at you right now.'

'Mum, why . . . you . . . I . . . never mind. If you're not going to punish me, what are you going to do?' I really was confused that she wasn't even punishing me.

'Nothing.'

Monday 11th, 6pm

Mum was really annoyed with me. I could tell she was. I never thought she would ever be this mad with me though. I even tried speaking to her later, but she just rolled over on her bed. I then asked her what was for dinner and she told me to wait and find out. This was the worst she had ever been with me. Well, apart from the shoplifting. But that was something that I did for her.

'Teve, why Mummy mad wif you?' Laura must have been so confused.

'I don't even want to talk about it.' Laura was looking at me with her pondering eye. It was confusing me as well!

'It's dinner time, Laura,' said Mum, obviously not including me.

Laura skipped off into the kitchen quite merrily. I knew Mum wouldn't want anything to do with me for at least a couple of days. I decided to do something about it.

'Mum, I am going to tell you this whether you want to hear it or not. If you could read my mind you would know that things between us aren't right. I need you, I'm a loner without you.' I know I got some of it off the Offspring song 'I Want You Bad'. It is rather catchy though.

'Steve, I have waited so long to hear you say that to me! I love you so much, son. Just don't lie to me again or else you know what will be coming.' She came over to me and gave me the biggest hug ever.

Monday 11th, 8pm

Mum and me made up and Laura joined our hug. There was just one person missing - *Dad!*

'Mum, where's Dad?' I asked.

'He was called to a meeting, but he should survive,' she said in a joking way.

So now we are all okay and this had been quite a day. From nearly being robbed to forgetting to change into my clothes. I hope the rest of my days aren't quite like this!

Debbie Wynn (12)
Aith Junior High School, Shetland

A Day In The Life Of Rebecca Mills

Rebecca opened her eyes. She could hear the cockerel. She didn't want to get up, it was too cold. Wrapping her blanket around her, she sat up and heard her tummy rumble. Rebecca quickly put on her shoes. Her feet went numb with the cold. She stood up and made her way to her jacket and hat. She slipped them on and went outside. It was very cold, even though the sun shone over the hill.

She picked up two buckets and hung them onto a long, thin plank of wood. She hooked it over her shoulders and made her way along the path. When she reached the well, she dipped one of the buckets in, then the other. When the buckets were full of water, she hooked them back onto the plank of wood and walked back to the house. Rebecca took the buckets of water into the house and set them down on the floor.

Her father came through the door leading to the bedroom.
'Morning me lass,' he said, stretching.
'Morning Father. It's a bit nippy outside.'
Then her big brother, Jimmy, came through.
'Morning, Jim,' said Rebecca.
'Morning.' He walked over to the cupboard and took out a loaf of bread that their mum had picked up from the bakery the night before. He cut four slices and made two sandwiches for him and his father. He put them in a box and they set off.

Rebecca went over to the loaf. cut two slices and spread some butter on them. She lit the fire and sat down to eat her bread. Her mother came through.
'Your brother and sister are still asleep. Get them up as soon as you've finished your bread.'
'OK.' She finished her bread and woke them up.

They got their breakfast and went out to feed the hens and pigs. Rebecca stayed behind. She began to knit.

At teatime she made some tea for her brother, sister and herself. Her brother and sister went to the well to get some more water while Rebecca went to get hen eggs. When she came back she sent the children to collect more firewood.

'Go and get some firewood, the fire is dying down.'
When they came back, Rebecca gave them some supper and sent them to bed.

Her mother came in.
'You're right me lass, it is a cold day.' She made some vegetable soup and sat in front of the fire.

Rebecca's father and older brother came home when it was dark. They had some soup and went to bed.
'Rebecca, I think it's time we went to bed.'
Rebecca slipped off her shoes and walked over the cold floor to her bed. She got in beside her young brother and sister and she fell asleep.

Lauren Bulter (13)
Aith Junior High School, Shetland

A Day In The Life Of David Who?

David gets up at 7am. He goes to the kitchen and he gets himself a cup of tea. He then goes to get the kids up for school and then gets his wife up. David goes to the shop to get some food. He gets bread, milk and eggs. When he comes home, he cooks them all breakfast and then washes up. By this time it is 8am and this is when he goes to work to play football.

At 1pm he goes to the nearest café and gets himself a sandwich and a Coke. He goes to the local paper shop to buy the daily newspaper. After that he goes back to the training field to play football with the coach and the other team members. They play until 10pm, then he goes home and goes to bed.

Next day David gets up and watches TV all day because it is Friday and he loves to drink Coke and watch football. He also wants to go on holiday with his wife and kids to Spain.
It is now evening and he is watching Pop Idol. It is 7pm and they are having steak and chips. After dinner he plays with the kids and his wife. He puts the kids to bed and then he and his wife go to bed.

Anna Mackenzie (13)
Aith Junior High School, Shetland

A Day In The Life Of Me!

(Morning)
Get up at 8.35am, get dressed, go and get washed.

(Breakfast)
Go get a drink of orange juice, some cheesy toasties, some cereal or some toast.

(Morning)
Go to school at 8.50am. The minute I get into the classroom, Mrs Morris comes to the door. Asked the teacher if she could take me out of the class. She talks, either giving me trouble or asking me what kind of week I've had.

(Lunch)
Have a school dinner or go to detention and then go for my dinner. Then go in the music room and play the drums or base.

(Afternoon)
Go to class. Get in trouble.

(After school)
I either go to after school club, to the leisure centre or the shop and play with friends.

(Evening)
Have tea at house. Play PlayStation or go on Internet.

Gary Lockyer (12)
Aith Junior High School, Shetland

A Day In The Life Of Jamie Dobb

I woke up at about 9am and went downstairs, I put on the TV, watched for about 20 minutes and then went to get some breakfast. I went into the kitchen, got a frying pan, some bacon and eggs and some sausages. I fried them and had them for my breakfast. After that I went upstairs and put on my jeans and T-shirt. I then went to the bathroom and brushed my teeth.

I went outside at about 10am, put my motorbike into the truck and my 5ft ramp. After I had done that, I went into the living room and played on the PS2 for about an hour.

At about 1pm I set off in the truck with my motorbike and ramp in it. We went to the racetrack. I unloaded the bike but I didn't need to bring the ramp out because there were already loads there. I went over to the sandwich bar and got a turkey and salad sandwich and a can of Coke. After I had finished that, I took my motorbike and had a practise run around the racetrack.

At about 3pm I went onto the starting grid with my motorbike and started to race against other people. On the first lap I was third, but then the guy in front of me fell off while he was doing a jump. At about the fifth lap I overtook the person who was first. I won the race at last and I had a really good time.

After I had won the race, I drove back home and that was about 6pm. I ordered an Indian take away. This is the one I love best and my favourite meal is probably chicken tikka.

That evening I went to the cinema and then to the pub. I spent most of the night there.

I came home from the pub at about 2am I think. My girlfriend said I was completely out of it. I had a reason to get drunk, which was that I had won the race.

This was my day, so goodbye and drive safely.

Lewis Garrick (12)
Aith Junior High School, Shetland

A Day In The Life Of Spot

The family get up, have their breakfast and then let me out. For breakfast I have some dog food and bread. I drink water or sometimes milk.

I watch as Jet has his breakfast and then he rests for a while. I make him play with me. The children come out a little later. When they speak to me, I get a little, tingly feeling inside. They say things like, 'Good little boy.'

Then their mum calls them in and the farmer comes out to feed me. By this time I'm really hungry. Jet gets fed too. We bathe, get two slices of bread, some watery food and some dried food.

The children come out and start running around. Me and Jet start running too. We have a great time playing with the children and we play for ages.

The children get tired and go inside for something to eat. I think they call it tea. We get fed too. We have wet food, a piece of bread and some milk. The children don't come out again, so I chase after sheep, or geese, or sometimes the hens.

Before I go to bed, I get a piece of bread and some water. I eat the bread in bed. I don't go to sleep straightaway, I sit and bark out of the window at the moon. I get tired so I lie down. I hear the children go and then the farmer feed the hens. I go to sleep and dream about what might happen tomorrow.

Fiona Morrison (12)
Aith Junior High School, Shetland

A Day In The Life Of . . . Me!

Every morning I get up at 7am, watch TV for a few minutes and then get dressed. I go downstairs and everyone except me has breakfast. To be honest, I think that breakfast is a waste of time and I can never be bothered to have it anyway.

At about 8.15, me and my brother, Matthew, get picked up at the end of our road and go to the bus that takes us to school. The bus journey can get kind of boring sometimes, but to pass the time I talk to my friends. Sometimes we can have really weird conversations that don't really mean anything.

The first two periods of the day are really annoying and I can hardly stay awake because I am so tired. After break it's not so boring because I have usually woken up by then.

Lunchtime is really cool because I get my lunch and then I usually go into the music room to play my electric guitar, or I go into the computing room to play Age of Empires against my friends. If I'm not allowed in the music or computing room, then I just talk with my friends or go outside to play football.

The afternoons are probably the best time of the day because I usually can't wait to go home. What also makes the afternoons cool is that we usually have craft and design where we make stuff or we have home economics where we get to either make stuff or cook things.

The bus journey home is quite cool because I am glad that I am on my way home and I can't wait to get there. I have my tea at about 5pm. After tea I go outside and play football with my brothers Matthew and Cameron, and Scott sometimes tries to play as well. If I don't want to play football, then I go down into the village to skateboard with my friend Adam, and Andrew comes sometimes.

In the evening I watch EastEnders and two episodes of The Simpsons. At about 8.30 I go on MSN Chat to talk to my friends. Then I go on the Internet to either download things or to look for cheats for my PS2. Usually, at about 10pm I play my electric guitar for about half an hour. I finally go to bed at about 11 or 11.30pm after I have had a shower, then I watch TV until I fall asleep.

Darren Hodge (13)
Aith Junior High School, Shetland

A Day In The Life Of Christina Aguilera!

I woke up today at 7am with my alarm. I went through to the bathroom and had a shower then spent an hour trying to decide what to wear. I finally chose a pair of black leather trousers with a pink tank top.

When I came downstairs I could smell the most wonderful smell. My butler had made me a lovely breakfast with tea, toast, cereal and bacon. I really enjoyed it.

As I finished breakfast, I heard a horn toot. It was my limo. I grabbed my handbag. When I opened the door, there were thousands of fans outside with cameras and banners saying, 'We love you, Christina'.
Then I shouted for James and Rick, my two bodyguards. They came to the door and took me to the limo.

When I got to the studio, the lights and everything were all set up for my photo shoot. I had to change into 10 different outfits throughout the morning for the photos, dancing and singing.

By this time it was 1.30pm so I thought I would go for lunch, so I called on James and Rick. I finally found them so we set off to my favourite restaurant called Petit Le Jo. I had a great lunch, it was delicious.

I went shopping after that and bought a new pair of shoes. They were black and very chunky. I also bought a new outfit. The top and trousers were yellow with black writing on the trousers.

In the afternoon, I went to the big shopping centre where I had to sign autographs for fans. I had a lot of photos taken and my hand was sore from writing. It was good fun though and I was there till 6pm.

When I got home, my butler had made me the most fantastic meal ever. There were potatoes, vegetables, meat, gravy and all the extras. For pudding I had chocolate cake and a cup of tea.

I watched television for about an hour. Then I went to my music room to work on my new song, 'Beautiful'. I was sitting there for about two hours. After that, I went to my very own gym and worked out for about an hour.

At 10.30, I got ready for bed, but I never went to bed. I watched a film instead. It was 3 hours long so I eventually got to bed at 1.30am.

Aimee Keith (12)
Aith Junior High School, Shetland

A Day In The Life Of Meg Harvey (A Model)

Meg Harvey got up at 7am and had a shower, which lasted half an hour! She took 20 minutes to choose what to wear, but she finally decided on her 5 inch, knee-length leather boots and her denim mini skirt. She chose a nice, blue gypsy top and left out her denim jacket for later. She then went into the bathroom and did her hair and make-up.

Meg went downstairs and made a cup of tea. She grabbed an apple, finished her breakfast and went to get her jacket. At 8.50 she went to work.

At 9.15, Meg had a meeting with some fashion designers. They showed her some sketches of some new designs. She got measured for the clothes for the catwalk and her photo shoots she had later. She tried on some of the clothes as well.

She met up with some of her friends (they were models too). They went to a little café called 'Little Charlie's'. Meg had her usual cup of coffee and a salad. When they were all finished, they went to do some photo shoots. The photo shoots started at 2.30pm.
When they were all done, they went for their tea. Meg had a bowl of low calorie soup.

At 6.30 they had to get ready for the catwalk. They had their hair done nicely and the make-up artist put on a lot of make-up. They got their new clothes on and at 7.30 they were ready for the catwalk. The show went well and Meg was finished at 10.30.

After a hard day's work, Meg was completely tired out and she got to bed at 11pm.

Lauren Walterson (12)
Aith Junior High School, Shetland

I WAS JACKIE CHAN

I got up and got dressed. Then I started to cook some noodles. Then, before I knew it, a demon smashed through my window. The demon had me cornered, so I ran up the wall and backflipped over him. Then I kicked his ass and ate the noodles in the car on the way to the film set.

That morning I did some stunts, ran up some walls, killed some bad guys - all the normal stuff. It was a bit boring.

I had lunch with the director. We had crispy duck and spare ribs with egg fried rice. In the afternoon I had to run down a 50-foot building. I was very nervous about it, but when I did it, it was great fun. I got to leave work early, so I went for a massage.

Suddenly, a demon smashed through the roof. I rolled off the bed and as the demon landed on it, I pushed it out of the window.

I headed for home, ate a Pot Noodle and then went to bed. A demon smashed through the ground. I let out a groan and fell asleep.

Kristian Fraser (12)
Aith Junior High School, Shetland

A Day In The Life Of Kelly Osbourne

Kelly Osbourne gets up early on days she's in the studio and sleeps in when it's the weekend or school. She has pink everything, her pjs are pink and sometimes her hair is pink. She has cereal most days (Cheerios). She and Jack fight over who gets what and who has that. She has a bathroom in her room so she uses that shower when she goes for one. Her room is very clear most days. Her bed is pink, it is a four-poster. The covers are pink, her walls are pink as is nearly everything in her bedroom.

Most of the morning is busy for Kelly. She sits around on days when she isn't doing anything, and it is hectic on busy days. She is more organised than her brother, Jack. She likes animals, she feeds them and takes them for walks.

When it comes to lunchtime, she gets some friends together and they go out for lunch. Afterwards she goes shopping. She uses her dad's credit card. When she comes home her mum tells her she will be in for it when Ozzy sees his bill next month . . .

In the afternoon she goes to the studio. Last Friday she was in London recording, 'Papa Don't Preach' for Top of the Pops.

For tea she will have something quick, not a big family dinner, a TV dinner or a microwaved dinner. On Sundays they might try to have a Sunday roast.

After tea Kelly watches TV with Jack or Mum. Kelly likes the Kerang! music channel. On hot summer nights she likes to go swimming in their outside pool.

I don't think Kelly sleeps in her bed much. She loves clubbing and parties. She goes out with friends and might not be back till the early hours of the morning. She is also on tour so she will get to sleep on the bus or the plane.

Inga Tulloch (13)
Aith Junior High School, Shetland

SPONSORS FOR COMIC RELIEF!

Comic Relief, 14th March 2003, has had so many sponsors this year even from schools! Ash Green's 7SP students, Shane Green and Steven Hall say that they are coming to school wearing their non-uniform clothes backwards and inside-out. Will they be comfortable enough to do it? Jody Tague and Victoria Henry say that they are coming to school wearing their pyjamas, dressing gowns, socks and slippers. Will they be warm enough or even brave enough? Nicola Hammond and Emma Moore say that they are not going to talk for a whole day! Will they be able to keep their mouths shut for a whole day? What about the register? If you want to sponsor any of these children, please visit or phone Ash Green Secondary School!

Red Noses are also available at Ash Green for £1

Help raise money for Comic Relief, please!

Megan Hyde (11) & Zoe Green
Ash Green School, West Midlands

My Day With Henry VIII

I woke up one morning to find that the bed underneath me had collapsed. I felt hungry. I went to the bathroom to wash my face when suddenly there was a massive *bang*, only to find it was King Henry VIII. I quickly locked the bathroom door so he didn't come in. Then, suddenly, he started shouting and screaming for me to open the door. *Crash!* He smashed the door down and stared into my eyes in a furious way. He grabbed my hair and chucked me out of the door. I was furious so I blurted out, 'At least I am not fat like you!'

Then, strangely enough, he just ran straight past me into the kitchen and started stuffing his face with fatty food. He came back up the stairs and got dressed but nothing fitted him because all the buttons had flicked off.

Anyway I went for a tour around the house and I came to his bedroom. I found loads of heads in massive bottles with water in them. I said, 'Who are they?'
He said, 'They are all of my six wives' heads.'
I asked him why he had got them. He said they were for a presentation.

That was my day with the fearsome King Henry VIII.

Chanice Relton (11)
Ash Green School, West Midlands

A Day In The Life Of My Cat

Dear Diary . . . please help me . . .

Oh God, I never get any peace with her always picking me up! I've only got 4 more lives to go then I'm history! But at least I'll be away from this household.

Oh here we go again. When are they going to lay my food down? Oh, here she comes with her feet clapping against this rock-hard marble, freezing cold floor. I wonder what I've got, probably something mingy that she's laid down. Ah well, see you later, I'm going to have my unsuitable tea. Bye . . .

An hour later . . .

Dear Diary,

I knew it, I knew it, didn't I tell you it wouldn't be my favourite food. Fish! I hate fish, it's just not my food.

Oh no, here we go again, the dog, that stupid dog, always making me jealous, but when I give her the evils she starts chasing after me. She's like a galloping horse being an idiot who's always chasing after me! She's just so dumb!

Two days later . . .

God, this girl, she's after me this time - I'm gonna lose my temper in a minute. I'm in a bad mood and I'm gonna scratch her. *She's squeezing me. I've only just eaten my dinner! God help me . . I think I'm gonna be sick, blurrrrh!*

Kyrie Gallagher (12)
Ash Green School, West Midlands

HERCULES AND RANDALL, DEMON OF THE SEA

Hercules swam into the dull and miserable cave of Randall. As he broke the surface he took a few desperate gasps of air. He climbed on a slippery rock. He moved slowly, very slowly. He twisted and turned round a tight, narrow corner which was pitch-black.

Hercules, never knowing where he was stepping, was waiting in case Randall appeared. He stopped immediatley and drew his shimmering silver sword and swung it behind him. Hercules followed a bright light. At the end of the cave, he heard a hideous laugh. As he got closer it got louder.

He jumped in, sword out. Randall looked. Hercules turned, knowing if he looked he would be turned to ice. He jumped out of the way. He ran straight towards Randall. His sword landed in his eye. Hercules ran out of the cave and swam to King Neptune who ruled the sea once again.

Jamie Brassington (11)
Ash Green School, West Midlands

HANNAH AND HER PUPPY

A little girl called Hannah had a little puppy called Max. Max and Hannah were very happy until they went on holiday.

In the car on the way to the airport, Hannah kept saying, 'Are we there yet? Max is getting hungry.'
'Not yet, just a few more miles,' her parents replied.

At the airport there were planes and lots of people climbing on aeroplanes and people shouting to other people. When they got out of the car, Max chased a cat all the way home.

At the airport, Hannah was crying and saying, 'Where's my dog? I want my dog.'

At home, Max was sitting on the front doorstep growling and barking and scratching to get into the house . . .

Emma Moore (11)
Ash Green School, West Midlands

HONEY, I'M HOME

Tonight people will be glued to their television screens. Tonight the evil Richard Hillman returns. Gail will realise that Richard takes his wedding vows very seriously, 'Till death do us part'. What will he do? We know he captures his wife, Gail. Tied up in his car are his step family, Sarah, David and Bethany.

Richard tells his family, 'If we can't be together in life, then we will be together in death.'
Will they all die? Reports are that Richard will be pulled out of the canal dead, but who else will be killed? Let's hope Gail survives so she can maybe marry Ashley. Let's hope Sarah lives so she can have a family of four by the time she is twenty, and David has to survive. Who else in the street flares their nostrils like a mad pig? And poor Bethany, She has to survive so she can grow up happily in Coronation Street. Nobody else has!

Samantha Sanders (12)
Ash Green School, West Midlands

ALIEN INVASION

At midnight on June 19th, aliens invaded Earth because Earth had destroyed their planet, Mars.

They arrived by spaceship but more pods were to follow. There were over 5,000 highly trained aliens using a style of mortal combat to defeat the earthlings. The aliens started attacking people all over the world.

The aliens wiped out Britain and other countries were also being conquered. Half of the world was killed and 20 aliens were also killed.

Those people who were left went to build a new life underground. They took refuge in the miles of underground sewers that were built hundreds of years ago.

The aliens, thinking that they had totally wiped out the humans left of find another planet to inhabit. May God help those who live on that planet!

Ben Morris (11)
Ash Green School, West Midlands

NEVER KEEP YOUR WINDOW OPEN

Hi, I'm Sam and I have a big problem. I'm fourteen and I'm still scared of the dark. Yesterday I went to bed and I couldn't get to sleep because all I could hear was the thunder and lightning outside. I was clutching my bunny when suddenly there was a power cut and all the lights went out. I started to get really worried. I could hear Mum downstairs asking Dad where the candles were.

A couple of minutes later, I heard a purring sound coming from my window. I noticed my mum had left my window open. Something had jumped into my room and it had knocked a load of books off the shelf. I clutched my quilt to my chest. I decided to try and find the door, when something crawled across my bed. I screamed for my mum and fell out of my bed. I was actually glad when lightning struck because it gave me light to see where the door was.

When Mum came upstairs she opened my bedroom door. The lights finally came on. 'Hurray,' I shouted.
Mum nearly fell over when she looked in my room. 'It's a mess,' she screamed.
'There's a monster in my room, Mum!' I said.
When we looked on the bed where the little purring thing was, it was next-door's cat, Jasper.
'Never keep your window open,' said Mum.

Adam Durran (12)
Ash Green School, West Midlands

My Discovery

The air was penetrating and bleak; the sky was inky and dismal. I felt a chill over my ashen cheeks. My school bag weighed down into my feeble shoulders. I scanned the sky for the moon, but there was no sign. My legs felt brittle and weak, I felt like collapsing, but I continued to walk. Missing the bus home was probably my greatest achievement today. My breath evaporated into the night sky. The road seemed empty apart from a couple of cars now and then. To be honest, I felt scared; terrified! I wasn't used to coming home this late at night. In fact, I really had no idea where I was going. Perhaps I was following the road to nowhere. Well, not really, I knew my way around the area roughly! My trainers crunched into the gravel as I approached the park. It was all too silent and eerie for me. I was too tired to go on so I decided to sit down. Suddenly, apart from what happened to be coming from behind the bush, were voices. Not just one or two, but maybe four or five. Silence. And that was that.

I got up from the bench and walked towards the spot where I thought the sound was coming from. I dragged my feet against the rough earth, it was then that my foot hit something. At first, I didn't really know what to expect, but it occurred to me that it was a box. Just an ordinary box. I knelt down to where it lay and brushed the earth from it. I didn't know whether I should open it or not, but before a thought could pass through my head, I lay my hands over the wooden clasp of the box. I flung it open. Inside lay the most beautiful necklace I had ever seen. The white stones flickered and glittered in the night sky.

I picked up the box and shoved it into my rucksack. As I walked home, I thought about what I had found. Rightfully, it was not really mine, but whose was it? As soon as I got home, I rushed straight to my room where I switched on my PC. I was halfway through checking my e-mail when it suddenly came to me that there must have been something important about this necklace, otherwise, the people whom had it before me wouldn't have hidden it! Since I was already online, I decided I would try to find out as much as I could about this necklace. I opened my rucksack and pulled it out. I fingered the clasp of the box and let it free. I held the necklace to the light, looking for anything, anything at all. And there they were, just nine regular numbers. '727996793'. They must have meant something. I looked it up on the Internet and there it was. *Eureka!* There were two sentences that sent shockwaves running through my mind.

'Stolen in 1953 from the Al-Senko jeweller store in Greece, it is the most valuable jewellery piece in Europe. It is worth an amazing £3m, and is made of pure platinum and white diamonds.'

Hey, hold on a minute! I remember my mum telling me about something about her childhood stories in Greece, and I recall something about her father having a jewellery store in there too! Could it be? I could only find out. I rushed back downstairs and called my mother. I asked her to tell me the story again.

She said, 'Your grandfather used to have a shop called the Al-Senko, in the centre of Greece.'

From that day onwards, I knew that it *was* rightfully my necklace. And I will end by saying, 'A little bit of family history, can bring you a long way!'

Hafsah Ahmed
Islamia Girls' School, London

A Day In The Life Of A Lock

On Thursday 18th October, I became a lock for the day and this is my story . . .

I lay there, all rusty and brown. The wind whirled around me as I waited to be noticed. I felt small. I felt like an ice cube waiting in a freezer for someone or something to come and put me into their sweltering, mouth-watering fluid.

It was unusual because I didn't eat. I've never spent a day in my own, natural life without eating. There was a gap in my daily routine. Other than that, everything seemed pretty natural.

I forgot all about food but there still seemed to be something missing. I was lonely. It took me some time to realise it. I was alone. I had no friends or family around me.

Suddenly there was a noise from the garden. Someone was coming, someone had thought about me. This made me feel special. But, when they came, they disappointed me. They didn't care about what I did for them. As long as their property was protected, they didn't care. He shoved his key in my lock, twisted it without a care in the world and took me off my hanger. The giant opened the gate, brought in his bike and pushed me back on.

Nothing happened after this, though. I became a loner once again. Hours passed and I knew my newly created life would soon be over. If anything good has come of this day, it is that I now appreciate my friends and family more. This is because I have realised the importance of their role in my life.

Tanya Collier (12)
Joseph Leckie Community School, West Midlands

THE MORGAN GUARDIAN
NEW CREATURE FOUND!

Excitement has taken over the town of Walsall today, as a new creature has been found. Seven girls on their way to science found it. Their names are: Perri Harris, Melissa Westhead, Symran Khangura, Katie Morgan, Kendall Russell, Rachel Aston and Catherine Wade.

The girls are delighted to have been able to name the creature; the eventual name was *'The Leckie Creature'*. It's odd name, however, is nothing to its appearance. It has rainbow-coloured fur with seven pink antennae. It has ten silver and gold legs and its body is oval shaped.

'It is a great honour to have been able to have found a creature, especially in your home town!' exclaims Melissa Westhead at an interview at Joseph Leckie CTC where the creature was found.

'It's amazing to have found such an extraordinary creature in such an ordinary town!' cried Cathy Wade at the same interview.

All seven girls are to be interviewed by David Attenborough and be featured in several news programmes followed by a *Wildlife on One* special.

The creature is currently being sent off to Oxford University for lab tests.

Katharine Morgan (12)
Joseph Leckie Community School, West Midlands

STARS PERFORM AT LOCAL SCHOOL

A local school is having a special 'celebrity day' when six of the school's favourite celebrities will come and do some sort of performance. These celebrities are: Matt Jay, James Bourne and Charlie Simpson, all part of the most voted band, Busted, Lee Ryan, Duncan James, Antony Costa and Simon Webb from Blue, Justin Timberlake, Prince William, David Beckham and Christopher Parker aka Spencer Moon in EastEnders.

Six lucky pupils will win a day and night out with each star. Busted, Blue and Justin will perform a gig especially for the school and each student will receive a signed album from their favourite singer out of that group.

David Beckham will teach his latest football skills in a very special PE lesson, and Christopher will be giving acting tips and doing some drama. Prince William will be joining in with the sports as he will play a game of rugby with selected pupils.

It looks like the students are in for the greatest school day ever.

Sarah Ashcroft (12)
Joseph Leckie Community School, West Midlands

THE KHANGURA EXPRESS - WICKED WITCHES AND WIZARDS STRIKE AGAIN FOR THE 5TH TIME

It was announced yesterday that another Harry Potter book will be released on 21st June 2003.

The title of the forthcoming book is *Harry Potter and the Order of the Phoenix*. The proud author, J K Rowling, said, 'The last four books were a huge success and I am positive that this one shall be no exception'.

This announcement is making the public go wild. Most book stores such as Waterstones and W H Smith are already reserving books for when the fantastic book is released.

Harry Potter and the Order of the Phoenix is said to be bigger and better than ever.

More Harry Potter books are being released in the near future along with more movies.

Symran Khangura (12)
Joseph Leckie Community School, West Midlands

THE SINGING ELEPHANTS

Long ago, where elephants had long tails and short noses, stood the Shelly Resident Stable. Here lived two lively and energetic elephants named Nelly and Kelly. 'Oh Nelly,' shrieked Kelly, 'I'm so nervous, how's my tail?'
'Stop worrying, Kelly, everything's going to be fine, and I'm sure we'll win,' advised Nelly.
'Come on, I can hear Bob the manager calling us.'

After the show, Bob started to explain a major issue to the twins.
'I've heard you lie and boast to your friends. This will spoil your career and all elephants shall suffer a punishment. I shall now send my fairy friend, Tinkerbella to watch over you, now go!'

A year went by and Nelly and Kelly did something they shouldn't have. It all started in the park. They were sitting under a large oak tree. Suddenly their friend, Fred came rushing towards them.
'Guess what, my manager has increased my salary. I now get forty peanuts instead of twenty *every day!*' shouted Fred with excitement.
Nelly, who was burning with greed yelled, 'Well Kelly and I get seventy peanuts *each* every day!'
Kelly joined in with all the lying and boasting. Immediately after this, their noses went *longer* and their tails went *shorter.*

The twins were embarrassed. Nelly couldn't believe that her lovely tail had gone!

From then the twins never lied. They made lots of friends and were world famous. They had a lovely career.

That is why, to this present day, elephants have long noses and short tails.

Moral: Never lie!

Aaisha Sidat (12) & Aysha Sidat (12)
Joseph Leckie Community School, West Midlands

The Grandfather Clock

Hi, my name is Tim, Tim Ravette. I've got red hair and green eyes and I'm about 5 feet tall. I shall be telling you about a very strange but fantastic grandfather clock I came across a month ago.

My mum, my brother Steve and I were walking down our local high road one afternoon, when my mum noticed that *Anthony's Antique Store* had a sale on, and decided to take a look. When we got in, I felt a strange tingle of excitement come over me as I looked around seeing all the great places to hide if I were playing hide-and-seek.
Steve said, 'Let's play hide-and-seek, I'll go first, you hide.'
So I rushed off into the far left corner of the store.

That's when I saw it, the most magnificent grandfather clock ever. It must have been at least 2 metres tall, made from pure mahogany; it had a gold trim around the frame and clock face. It took me no time at all to jump in and stand behind the pendulum, when I heard from the front of the store, '9 . . . 10, Tim, I'm coming for you!'
So I quickly shut the door and there was a big, bright, blue, blinding flash.

When I could see again, I looked past the pendulum and through the glass in the door expecting to see Steve looking for me. He wasn't there. Not only wasn't he there, but it seemed that I wasn't in the store anymore either, but I was now in a kind of jungle.

I stepped out of the clock feeling scared, especially after I looked up to see large flying dinosaurs and a herd, of what I thought were dipolodocus, walking in the distance.

I decided to explore the area, and, after seeing some amazing flowers, I was startled by a tap on the shoulder. When I turned round, I was shocked at what I saw. It was almost the spitting image of myself, wearing a tigerskin loincloth. He looked at me and said, 'Hi ug, I'm Jim Rockette, uga og, did your ag ug dad send you ug out hunting too?'
'No, but do you need help?' I gasped.
'Uuuuug, yep, if you ug don't mind!'

So I spent an hour trying to catch what he called a chickomocus, which happened to look like a chicken. I caught 2 but Jim, the expert, caught 6.

As I was taking some back to Jim's cave, a dinosaur with a thorny, clubbed tail jumped out of a bush in front of us. I was just about to scream in terror and run, when Jim told me not to speak or move, because it was a blindosaurus and it had remarkably bad eyesight. The problem was that it had devastatingly good hearing and could sense movement. When it moved on, I let out a great sigh of relief and said goodbye to Jim and stepped back into the clock.

Once I had shut the door, there was once again a big, bright, blue, blinding flash. When I could see again, all I could see was darkness. Then I heard, 'Tim, come on, get up!'

It was my mum and as I lifted the quilt the darkness faded. I looked around. I was in my bedroom in my bed, and I was wearing my dinosaur pyjamas with my dinosaur duvet, and then it hit me. *It was all a dream!*

Matthew A Hector (13)
Langdon School, London

SHORT STORY ON NEWSPAPER ARTICLE

We're here in Iraq reporting for CFG News. Our team leader, Terry has got us here against all odds. We have witnessed the Americans killing many innocent civilians and also many surrendering Iraqi troops. The Americans are very rough; their gun happy soldiers would kill anything in their way. We have filmed extraordinary scenes; Iraqi villages hit by fierce bombing but these were to be the last of our group leader, Terry's life. He was shot in an extraordinary, unexplained attack.

As surrendering Iraqi troops on the road to Basra approached us, a line of American tanks opened fire on the group, killing most and leaving the rest for dead. Terry, a front seat passenger in one of the jeeps was killed instantly. He was in the direct line of fire. His body is in hospital in the nearby town of Basra, still a battle zone. I only survived after throwing myself from the burning jeep into a nearby ditch. It was there that reporter, Melanie Smith found me. The American army deny the charges against them, but we can now reveal that CFG has identified Terry's body from video footage. One frame clearly shows the wound in his head. He died instantly. He was in the passenger seat when they opened fire setting alight the petrol cans on the jeep's roof. I was crouching under the steering wheel, I looked up just before we crashed and Terry was gone. Terry described the war as being a great hardship to the Iraqi people, there was no way of knowing that it was to bring him the greatest hardship of all.

Sohail Mohammed (12)
Langdon School, London

THE FINAL KICK

It's the last minute of the game and the Eagles are drawing one all with the Lions in the Cup Final and Smith steps up for the Lions to take a well deserved penalty. If he scores, the game is all over for the Eagles and the Lions will win their second cup this year.

Everyone is screaming for him to score. What must be going through that young man's head! The coach of the Eagles is on the sideline arguing with the referee about the penalty that was given. He reckons that it shouldn't have been a penalty.

What's this? The referee has sent the coach off and out of the stadium. This is a thrilling match.

Smith and the Eagles' goalkeeper are staring each other out, but it looks to me as if Smith is winning the staring competition.

The referee comes back on the pitch to blow the whistle for the penalty. Smith puts the ball on the penalty spot staring at the goal. Will he score?

The referee puts the whistle in his mouth, staring at his watch. Smith takes one look at his coach and nods his head. The referee blows the whistle and Smith runs up to take the penalty. He swings his foot to the left, but the ball goes to the right and completely tricks the goalkeeper who dives to the left. What a goal!

The coach runs onto the pitch grabbing hold of Smith and lifting him up. The cup has been won by the Lions for the second year running.

What a game of football! And now I say goodbye from me, Christopher Worby from Eagles United football stadium.

Christopher Worby (12)
Langdon School, London

ILLUSION

'You may enter now.'

Ray took one final glance in the mirror, his mop of crimson hair spilled over his face and there were bags underneath his azure eyes. He had spent the past few weeks studying the arcane arts and now he would have to complete his first spell unaided.

'You may enter now,' repeated the headmaster.

'As you wish,' replied Ray as he stepped through the door into the room.

'Sit down,' commanded the headmaster as he indicated to an empty seat. 'Second page,' he diverted Ray's gaze to a book in front of him.

Ray opened the book and turned to the second page. It was an invisibility spell. 'Look at the glympth, really look at it until it is embedded in your mind,' the headmaster instructed Ray. Ray stared at the glympth until he thought his eyes would fall from their sockets, but he still continued, not once looking away.

After some time the intricate spirals that made up the glympth rooted themselves into his mind. Ray then closed his eyes, yet still seeing the glympth, he poured his manna into it. He was careful not to pour too much as it could be dangerous.

After he completed that, he released the spell and opened his eyes . . . he saw his hand. He wanted to cry out but he noticed that the headmaster was smiling and he turned to look into the mirror. He could not believe his eyes.; he was invisible. He had really done it. He was a wizard. Ray got up, shook the headmaster's hand and left for a well-earned rest.

Adil Rahman (12)
Langdon School, London

A Day In The Life Of David Beckham

1st May

I woke up this morning and I seemed very tired after last night's football game. I very quickly got changed and had a bath, it was cold. After breakfast I had to drop Brooklyn at his football club. I think his club is brilliant. I wish I were still Brooklyn's age. After I saw Brooklyn go onto the pitch, I went to Rio Ferdinand's house. He is a good buddy of mine. It was a very cold and breezy morning. We went to our favourite restaurant, McDonald's. We had to talk about a few football tactics. I dropped Ferdinand home and went home myself. When I got home I had to change Romeo's nappy, *poo!*

2nd May

Today my manager had called me up for one-to-one training. We have this every month. It got boring so I called my teammates and played a little 5 a side game. That was a laugh. I fell a few times, but no injuries. Victoria called me to ask what I wanted to eat; I was a bit embarrassed so I said I wasn't sure.

3rd May

Today I am getting ready for a meeting with Michael Owen. Michael Owen sometimes makes me feel like a 'not so good' football player. I went in a limo and I took Brooklyn with me. We talked about our national team and had lunch. It was delicious.

Mohammed Akram (13)
Langdon School, London

JOYRIDE

'Can you slow down? You can hardly see through the fog. What's wrong?'
'It's my step-dad, he's trying to control me and Mum doesn't care.'
'So you stole his car.'
'Borrowed.'
'We should go back home. Where are we? This place looks deserted, there isn't another car on the road. Pull over, we'll wait until the fog clears.'
'We can't just sit here, we have to find shelter.' Jason said, as he slowly pulled over.
'There's a house, it looks empty. Let's stay there.' They got out the car and ran to the door. They knocked, the door slowly creaked open.
'Hello, anybody home? Come on, I need to take my shoes off, they're wet.'
They looked around, it was dark, empty, dusty, old and shabby with cobwebs everywhere.
'We'll have to sleep on the table or floor, because there's no furniture,' Natalie said, as she climbed onto the table. She suddenly felt cold, a force pushed her off the table.
'Are you okay? I have a bad feeling about . . .' The force dragged Jason across the room, it lifted him and threw him onto a mirror. He sat up and looked at a broken piece of glass and saw something. Something evil. It wasn't clear, whatever it was.

Jason grabbed Natalie and ran towards the door. The door wouldn't open. They screamed for help and banged on the door. They started hearing footsteps coming towards them. They ran to the window, smashed the glass and climbed out.
'My sock's caught, help me Jason.'

Jason pulled her sock off. They ran and jumped into the car. Jason was shaking as he put the key in. They heard the footsteps again, but the car wouldn't start.

'Hurry up!'

He turned the key again, the engine started and he drove off as fast as he could.

Samba Kabwe (14)
Langdon School, London

WAKING UGLY

Once upon a time there was a girl, an ugly, horrific girl called Waking Ugly, who could never go to sleep because the pillow would always try to run away from her face. Not only did the pillow find her horrible, everyone did!

One day, a lovely, pure-hearted fairy, all beautiful, brought Waking a spinning wheel. But the daft cow pricked her finger on it and, afraid of infection, she fainted for a hundred years. No one really cared about her so they all left the palace to be deserted while the garden trees overgrew and turned wild.

One day a troll walked past and got suspicious about what he thought the palace and plants were hiding. So he used his crusty, big nails to cut all the plants down as he really wanted to possess the palace. To his amazement, he saw a troll queen (or so he thought, after all, she was really ugly).
'Wow, a royal troll,' he whispered, oblivious to the fact that she was human. He walked towards her and planted a big, fat, slimy, wet, dribble-covered spit on her face.
'Aaah!' she woke up, screaming and shrieking at the sight looking down at her.
'You're not pretty yourself, my dear. Seeing as no one likes you and I'm single, let's go,' he replied.
'Hmm, might as well,' she said and walked off with her prince and lived happily ever after (or so we thought).

Ikram Samater (14)
Langdon School, London

A Day In The Life Of Victoria Beckham

I wake up and make myself some breakfast before the kids get up. I sit there, switch on the telly and guess what, or should I say guess who I see? Yes, myself, and again it's a negative comment about how I am an anorexic stick. But when I switch over to the other channel, I am seen as a fashion guru. How ironic!

Then I go and open the paper and I have been accused of spending £10,000 on a birthday party for my son, Brooklyn. I didn't even spend that on my wedding. These papers are full of lies and I can't believe people actually believe them.

This morning I have a hospital appointment for my youngest son Romeo, then, in the afternoon, I have a magazine interview. I don't live this glamorous life that most people think I live.

The other night we had a meeting about reforming the Spice Girls. Personally I think it will be a laugh. My husband, David, thinks it will take up all my time. After all, I am a mother of two.

I remember the days when I was a Spice Girl. The girls and I had so much fun but then everything changed when we got a bit older. The thing I enjoyed most was performing for our fans; that would give me such a buzz. I remember one time when we were performing and my heel broke. Usually I would have been embarrassed but that night I just carried on and changed after the next song.

Samina Karim (14)
Langdon School, London

ASTROLOGERS SHOCKED AS HALLEY'S COMET COMES EARLY

Astrologers were shocked yesterday, after seeing Halley's Comet earlier. They saw it yesterday whilst checking their daily comet movements.

They saw a large object fly across their telescopes and knew it was Halley's Comet because of its size.

They reported the sighting at 10am to the head of NASA, who double-checked the sighting. NASA reported back, confirming that it was really there and not a mistake. Nick Carter and Tony Ashton say it could have been hit by some debris, which has changed its course.

We interviewed both of the astrologers. Nick Carter said, 'Halley's Comet is no danger to Earth, it will just pass like it has been doing for so long'.

We also interviewed Tony Ashton for his view on their finding.

'I think this new course could mean an earlier sighting, such as every 25 years instead of 76 years years like usual'.

They also said that it was not coming towards Earth, but it was going to skim the atmosphere. It will be seen from Earth without a telescope and will appear like an iceberg in the air. It will also have other little pieces of rock flying beside it.

Khalid Jeeva (14)
Langdon School, London

HOW LIGHT CAME TO THE WORLD

Long, long ago, there lived only one person on the planet. His name was Jojey.

Ever since Jojey was young, he had always wondered why it was dark. He could just see where he was going and just about see what he was doing. One day Jojey decided to make a difference to his life and try to make the world a lighter place.

He climbed to the top of a tree and picked the brightest coloured mango that he could see. He thought that he could bring light, by throwing the bright mango into the sky. He thought it would stay there . . . he was wrong.

Jojey was almost out of ideas, when a firefly shot past his face. Jojey followed the firefly until he came to a whole swarm of them, which he caught and packed into a little parcel that he had made with some green leaves. He found the tallest tree and put the parcel at the top. Light still didn't come.

The Greek God Prometheus saw what Jojey was trying to do and realised that Jojey was a very determined young man and thought to himself how much he admired Jojey's perseverance. He decided to reward Jojey by placing a giant ball of fire in the sky, to light up his world.

With the gigantic fireball in place, light came to the world for the whole of eternity.

Sam Gray (14)
Langdon School, London

THE DAY IT CAME DOWN TO EARTH

Bang! Total destruction. No one knew what it was, but it had dug-out two-fourths of the ground and scared the living daylights out of the people. One man said, 'It's a creature from outer space'. Five minutes later the cops came, followed by the scientists, to figure out what it was and what the symbols read. The symbols read *'death'*. Everyone was shocked, no one exactly knew what to do, all you could hear was loud talking around the 'object'.

It finally opened, people gasped, most people stood still in fear, while others ran. A great beam of light went up into the air and a large figure popped out. It had green skin all over, red eyes and the sharpest teeth you have ever seen. One man shouted, 'What the hell is it?'

The creature made a noise that sounded like fingernails scraping a blackboard. Everyone covered their ears. The creature then pulled out a weird gun with a green ray coming out of it. It was being pointed at everyone that was there. The next minute, everyone was bowing. The creature then turned it into a red ray. Instantly fire broke out all around the place, big buildings were broken down and similar creatures started popping up everywhere from the ground. The sky turned black and misty. This seemed to be the end of mankind as we knew it.

Vijay Davdra (14)
Langdon School, London

A Soldier's Destiny

'Please, please don't make this harder than it already is. I have to, it's my duty,' I proclaimed. 'You cannot stop me and I won't let you. It's what I have to do. It's my destiny, a soldier's destiny.'

These were the last few words uttered from my lips, as I left my home, my family, my fiancée, to a world with no rules, but ruthless aggression. A world of war.

We had arrived at our location by air, but made the rest of our journey on foot, each of us was more than eager to fight. During the first few days into the war, battle was stiff; many soldiers had to be removed from the front line as they were incapable of handling the pressure of war. Many had died.

Terrifying days beheld our troops as the war proceeded into its fifth day. Enemy missiles had been launched at our camp, claiming many victims. Vast numbers of our soldiers had surrendered in the fear of death, even our commander, General Kane. This act of cowardice left our troops vulnerable to attack; we had no choice but to go for an all out war!

Our plan was to besiege the enemy in their own territory and capture their HQ. We arrived at the enemy's HQ and decided to enter. Suddenly, a gunshot was heard. I turned round. There was General Kane with two enemy militants. Before proceeding with his action, he said to me that he would tell my fiancée how much I loved her and then . . .

Habezur Rahman (14)
Langdon School, London

LOCH NESS MONSTER

I had heard about the Loch Ness Monster, but I had never taken any notice of the stories that went round. I thought it was a myth, told but not to be believed in. My belief of this mysterious creature didn't change, until I went looking for it. I wanted to prove this foolish city, that they were just as gullible as their past generation, who had believed in these ridiculous stories.

I went straight to the lake of Loch Ness, where this supposed monster was to be living. It was an isolated lake, cut off from the open sea by a range of low mountains. Even though it was cut off, it was surrounded by waves of trees and astounding plants, which swayed with the wind; as though they were alive. It was a paradise which no one appreciated and had left behind. Through all these dismal expressions it gave off, it had the beauty that no one had seen before. It was as silent as a graveyard; nothing moved; it was like nothing had ever existed to touch, or to see these tropical forests of heaven.

Suddenly, an immense rumble let out birds from the silent trees, which had once been so quiet and hand shown no sign of existence. The birds turned the sky into different colours of the rainbow.

The lake turned into a furious water whirl, then I saw the hideous creature glide slowly, trying to prevent itself from being seen. In and out of the water it weaved itself, changing the cool blue of the water to a ghastly green. For several seconds I stood there, shocked, not moving, not breathing. I moved towards the creature and stroked its rough skin.

Suddenly, the creature leapt up towards me. My legs felt like jelly and became useless. I stood there and then to my amazement, I was running. Running away from the horrid monster. Past the trees, past the unfamiliar hillsides. Somewhere I'd be safe. The wind brushed against my face, as I felt my hand sting in pain. I looked down at my hand and where normal skin should have been, was a swollen, wrinkled, blue hand.

Mariya Rashid (14)
Langdon School, London

MUGGED

My heart skipped a beat. I never thought this would happen to me, not at this age. I was 76 years old and was happily walking down the street to the grocer's, when I saw a peculiar car parking beside me. I didn't think anything of it, so I carried on walking. I turned around to look and saw the same car parked next to me. Then I started to have a funny feeling inside me. I decided to slow down and wait for the next person to come by, so that I could walk next to them, but no one was around. Then again, it was 8.45 on a Sunday morning and no one would be around. I started to pick up my pace, but I didn't get anywhere.

It was then it happened. They came up behind me and grabbed my handbag. It all happened so quickly. There were two of them, they were both dressed in black and had balaclavas on. One held me and the other grabbed my bag. He emptied out my bag, he picked up my purse and left my bag. In my purse was the only picture of my youngest son who had died when he was 14. Now, that too, had gone.

Amarpreet Kaur (14)
Langdon School, London

STRONG SAMSON

There was once an extremely strong man called Samson. Samson was part of a group called the Israelites. The Israelites had many enemies, the fiercest of which was the Philistines. Samson used to attack the Philistine soldiers and burn their crops and houses. The Philistine leaders were fed up with Samson and wanted to know the secret behind Samson's super-human strength.

They sent for a beautiful woman called Delilah and asked her to find the secret behind Samson's strength.
'Very well,' she said, 'but my fee is 1,100 silver coins.'
'That's OK, we don't care, as long as Samson is stopped,' said the Philistine leaders.

Delilah grew very close to Samson and asked him why he was so strong.
'I wouldn't be if you tied me with seven new bow strings,' laughed Samson.

When Samson was asleep, Delilah tied him up with bow strings. Samson broke free, with ease.
'But you said that . . .' screamed Delilah.
'I know,' stated Samson, 'but I really can't tell you.'

Delilah did not give up and eventually Samson told her that he was strong because his hair had never been cut. Whilst he slept, the Philistines cut his hair.

When Samson woke, his strength had completely gone.
'Where's your strength?' taunted the Philistines, as they put him in chains.

Months and months went by, with Samson laying in a cell. One day the Philistines took him to their temple, so everyone could see how weak he was. But the Philistines hadn't noticed that Samson's hair had started to grow back.

'Look at me, I'm stronger than ever!' shouted Samson, while destroying the temple and everyone in it.

Mandip Singh (14)
Langdon School, London

A Diary Entry Of A Bully Victim

Dear Diary,
I saw them again today. I tried to leave early so that they wouldn't see me, but I couldn't. I don't walk home with anyone anymore, because I don't want anyone knowing my secret. As soon as I saw them, I tried to hurry up, but they saw me and said, 'Oi! You little nobody! Why are you walking away from us?' I tried to walk on, but my legs wouldn't let me. So I had to turn round and face them. I wanted to say something strong and brave like, 'What do you want?' but I couldn't.

They said, 'Where were you all day? You're not trying to avoid us, are you?' I said nothing. I tried to ignore them, but then one of them punched me in the face. Then the stomach. Then the others joined in. I couldn't do anything about it. People looked and stopped for a minute, but then walked on. If only they knew.

If only they knew that every day I have to walk home battered and bruised because of those bullies. If only they knew that I had to hide in my room to cover my bruises. If only they knew the emotional trauma I suffer from because of these bullies. Nobody knows. I can't tell anybody. It has to be my secret. If I tell my friends they might say that I deserve it. Today I was lucky. Tomorrow is another day. Who knows what tomorrow may bring?

Christine Rodrigues (13)
Langdon School, London

LOCH NESS MONSTER

In the mysterious highlands of Scotland, a mythical creature lurks in the lake.

I arrived in Scotland, without knowing the boundaries of the Loch Ness. I stayed in a hotel in front of the lake. I didn't even think about wasting a minute. Minute! Not even a second!

Next morning, at dawn, I set out to do a survey on the Loch Ness monster. Local village people had said the same things, like 'The Loch Ness monster is very big and even, it's very vicious.'

After all my information, I was ready to go in search of the Loch Ness monster. Something was holding me back. I was very timid and alarmed of what I was about to do. So I stepped outside for fresh air. I glared into the lake. The atmosphere was very foggy and gloomy and it was impossible to see anything.

The following morning I remembered people had said the monster would be vicious. Vicious! I wondered if instead it would be very calm. I took an ultrasound with me to hear echoes. I put it in the sea and waited for an hour. Suddenly, something had bitten me, I screamed loudly. The local peopled shouted, 'Run! Run!'

I went to the hotel and cleaned all the blood off. As I was doing that, I thought to myself, *what was it that bit me? Could it have been the Loch Ness monster? Is the myth true after all?* I knew I would come back, but only time would tell!

Jahad Uddin (13)
Langdon School, London

THE VIRGINIA FOREST

Jean and her parents had decided to spend their weekend camping in the Virginia forests, where they would meet up with their friends.

On their journey to the forest, Jean wouldn't stop talking about how eager she was to meet her friend Penny, who she hadn't met for more than two years. As they got closer to the forest, the weather became very dark and dreary, the rain started to fall heavily and the wind started to blow harder than usual. The roads became empty and narrower.

They finally reached the campsite late in the night. They parked their car on the edge of the forest, next to the trees. By now, the rain had stopped, the wind wasn't blowing as hard and you could see the stars twinkling next to the full moon. They took out their belongings and a torch and walked deeper into the forest.

They had been walking for more than 15 minutes and it seemed unusually quiet. Their vision became very poor because the torch's batteries became weak. Suddenly, Jean heard a gasp from her mum. She ran towards her with the torch and saw that there were three dead bodies, one of which was her friend Penny. They were devastated at what they saw. Jean's dad said to get out of the forest quickly, so they started running. However, they got lost and to this day it is said that you can still hear them running in the forest, on a dark and dreary night.

Vibenche Yasocumaran (14)
Langdon School, London

GHOSTS OF MR AND MRS PETER

It was a really sunny day and I was feeling really tired and exhausted. It seemed like I had walked for miles, but I hadn't even walked past two streets. My leg was aching badly and I was dying for a gulp of water. After a few minutes more I saw a bench ahead of me, I ran to it and sat down. That was when I saw the ghosts of Mr and Mrs Peter.

At first I didn't notice them, but after a while I saw some silver liquid dripping from the gibbet. When I looked at this liquid carefully, I realised that it was blood. Then I saw the arms, the legs, the bodies and finally the heads, which looked more like a football.

Right at that moment I wanted to run, but my legs wouldn't move. I felt as cold as ice. I was scared of ghosts and had been since I was a kid. The only things that were on my mind were all those ghost stories that my gran used to tell.

I could not believe my eyes. I was so shocked and frightened. I could feel the sweat running down my spine and I felt really dizzy, as if I was going to faint. The next minute, I couldn't see anything, nor could I stand on my legs. I fell on my back and hit my head on the rock behind me.

Suddenly, I heard a familiar voice calling my name from a distance. It was my gran. When I opened my eyes, I was in my bed, safe and secure.

Elakkiya Sunthararajan (14)
Langdon School, London

MURDER AT NUMBER 37½

Don't worry, I'll get you, just you wait! That's all I could think about. I can still remember the anger in his eyes when he said that haunting phrase. I know he's dead, but I can still sense him. I know he's watching me. The only problem is, there's nothing I can do about it.

'Beverly! Can you go to the shop? I need some milk,' Mum called.
'Yeah, sure. I'll be down in a minute,' I replied. 'Do you want to come Tasha, then I can take you home afterwards?'
'Well, I suppose, but only if we're quick, I was supposed to be home 20 minutes ago.'

We decided to go down the alleyway as it saved five minutes. We were talking about Andrew, the world's most gorgeous boy, when all of a sudden we came to an end.
'Whoa, hold on a second Bev, we've gone too far.'
'No luv, it's always next to this house, number 37.'
'Not anymore, they must have built a new house in the short time we were in the shop. Actually come to think about it, I overheard someone talking on Tuesday about a haunted house, they call it number 37½. Oh, hold on, someone's ringing me. Hello, who's speaking?'

While Tasha was on the phone, I decided to open the gate.
'Er, yuck! Tasha there's paint all over the gate.' I turned to Tasha and she had a look of fear in her eyes. 'What's the matter Tash?' I asked.
'Th-th-that's not p-paint Beverly, it's b-b-b-blood,' she replied, looking as if she was going to faint, 'and it's not just anyone's blood. It's A-A-Andrew's. The guy on the phone told me. He knows who we are.'
'I hate to say this, but we're going to have to find out what's going on!' I whispered.

I dragged Tasha up the pathway leading to the front of the house, and found that the door was open. I slowly pushed it and we tiptoed in. I was scared. My knees were shaking but we had to help Andrew, even if he was half dead. Suddenly we felt two hands on our shoulders. We froze.
'Quick, in here! Before he comes.' Thank goodness it was Andrew.
'*Sshhh!* or he'll find us, and don't even think about asking what

happened to my arm.' Me and Natasha agreed on that. He was dripping with blood.

We heard some movement in the kitchen. Then we heard, 'Andrew, come back. I must have revenge!' in a lingering voice. At that moment I knew who it was and he was back. Jasper Jones! He was killed because of me and now he wants revenge.
'Atchoo!' Tasha sneezed.
He found us. Natasha and Andrew ran as fast as they could, leaving my foot trapped in a floorboard. I could sense him coming closer . . . and closer . . . and closer, until I could see a glimmer of a blade no bigger than a man's hand. Natasha turned around, she saw what was about to happen, then turned and ran out the front door, leaving behind only her little gold nose stud, which fell out when she sneezed. I know she heard my screams for help, but still she did nothing, just kept running with Andrew, as if it was a game.

I'll get you, just you wait and see! That's all Tasha can think about. She remembers the terror in her voice when Beverly said that haunting phrase. Tasha knows she's dead, but can still sense her. Beverly is watching her. The only problem is there's nothing she can do about it!

Jessica Manning (14)
Langdon School, London

CLIMBING MOUNT EVEREST

My rucksack is packed and I'm ready to go. My heart is racing and my nerves are coming into play. Everybody is cheering around me. The sun is shining like gold and the sky is clear. I can smell the fresh air around me. There she is. The humungous and the mightiest mountain in the world, Mount Everest. The closer I get to her, the more anxious I feel.

I start climbing, slowly but steadily. I turn around each time for encouragement from the crowd below me. After about eight hours, it is starting to get dark and my feet are excruciatingly painful. My rucksack is as heavy as lead and the pain in my back is agonising. I take a rest and watch the stars in the night. They sparkle in the dark sky like speckles of glitter.

The next morning, the sun rises and the sky is a beautiful orange. Afterwards the weather changes rapidly, the wind blows fiercely against me, it is as cold as ice as it hits my face. Nonetheless, I won't give up, not now, not after getting so far.

There, just above me, I see snow. It looks like the top. Yes, this is it! My heart rate is accelerating! I'm finally there. Oh great God! This can't be true! No, it just can't be true! it isn't snow, it is the clouds. As the clouds clear away, my fate is revealed. Mount Everest is victorious and has triumphed over me. It now looks like my journey will last forever.

Cinduja Surendran (14)
Langdon School, London

A DAY IN THE LIFE OF . . . A CAMEL

Saturday 29th March

I hate life! Why does it have to be so hard? I have to carry so many bundles on my back, with the sun scorching down on me.

Today was an extremely tiring and depressing day: my owner made me carry double the load that I usually do and we had to walk an extra three miles. We had to travel to another town, so we set off early in the morning and I hardly got any sleep.

There was a huge sandstorm today, which slowed us down. It made it hard for me to see and I couldn't walk as fast as my owner wanted me to. He kept on hitting me. He was lucky that he had lots of clothing on and sunglasses. Why doesn't he understand what I go through every day? I can only tell you and my friends.

We walked for a very long time and I was very thirsty; luckily we stopped at the oasis to have a drink - it also gave my legs a rest. When we got into town, I couldn't believe my eyes! There were so many other camels there, with their owners. I knew what it meant . . . an auction!

At the auction, many camels were bought. Only when it was time to come back and everyone was going; I saw my best friend, she had been bought and was going very far away. I couldn't believe it! This is the worst day of my life!

Priya Shah (14)
Langdon School, London

THE SCARECROW

It was on a cold night in November, when rain pattered on an old farmhouse in Devon. The fences of the deserted farmhouse were muddy and nearly falling over. The trees near the farmhouse had lost their leaves, due to the storm and the bark was softening.

On the farm was an old abandoned scarecrow. He had lots of hay, an old hat and he stood on a long, thin piece of wood. A bolt of lightning struck the scarecrow, leaving it damaged.

Later that night, two teenagers, aged 16, came walking past and noticed the abandoned scarecrow and they thought it would be funny to set him alight. As they were lighting the fire they suddenly noticed, that the scarecrow, which had been there before, was not there now and they ran off in terror.

The next day the two teenagers returned to find the scarecrow staring at them, face to face. This time the scarecrow had no hat and was standing against the farmhouse. People often said that the scarecrow looked scary and these two teenagers looked like they were scared. Then the weirdest and scariest thing happened. The scarecrow started walking towards them as if he was alive. The scarecrow then chased them and when he got them, he burned them alive. There were no traces of them left and no one saw the scarecrow do it.

Even today people say that the haunted scarecrow was a human and wanted to kill teenagers.

Khris Johal (14)
Langdon School, London

HERCULES

As his second labour, Hercules was ordered by Eurysteus to kill the many-headed Hydra of Lerna. Anyone who tried to kill it was ripped limb from limb. The swamp located in the south-east had evils that never slept and was so bad that Hades of the Underworld had to banish them to Earth.

On the way there Hercules and his nephew Iolas could not help but overhear what their mothers said about the Hydra.
'It has many heads and one immortal one,' said Iolas, depressed.
'We cannot track it, as its footprints are poisonous,' whispered Hercules as they approached the Swamp Of Lerna.
They drew breath, as that was the freshest air they were going to get. From here on the air was thick with smog and poisonous vapours.

Iolas discovered the cave where the monster lay.
'Stay outside Iolas! I'll call if I need you,' shouted Hercules, as he walked into the cave. As he entered the cave he felt heavy breathing upon his neck. Suddenly the Hydra sprung forth and forced Hercules' shield out of his hand. Hercules slashed and severed the hydra's heads but they grew back.

Iolas, torch in hand, came in on hearing the struggle and started singeing the necking of the hydra which stopped its heads from growing back. All that was left was the immortal head, but the hydra changed views and tore off Iolas' head within a second. Hercules, fuelled by his rage, hacked of the immortal head and buried it under a big rock along with his nephew.

Rajah Safrat
Langdon School, London

THE LIFE OF A DOCTOR

Wednesday 11th June 2002
Dear Diary

It was such a hard day today. I was supposed to be off duty but the hospital was running out of staff. Two of my colleagues called in sick and another is in hospital himself after a car accident. Anyway, getting to the point, in the hospital there were two boys around the age of 18 who were just involved in a fight. They had cuts and bruises all over their bodies and they were making a scene at the hospital too. They were a bit hard for me to control. So many people come in complaining of coughs and colds. I tell them that they can buy medicine from the chemist but unless they have breathing difficulties then I can't look at them. There's so much more to tell, but I'm too tired to write. I'll write tomorrow.

Thursday 12th June 2002
Dear Diary

Today was just a normal hospital day with the regular amount of patients and patience. I suppose there are good things about being a doctor, just this afternoon a woman came in saying she had stomach pain and when I told her she was three months pregnant she was so happy. When I told her about what would be happening to her in the next few months I felt proud of myself. Towards the end of my shift there were hardly any patients left, so they let me go early which meant I could spend some time with my son.

Friday 13th June 2002
Dear Diary

I went to work by train, well it is pretty far to work from where I live. Friday mornings are quite stressful because I have to sort out all the files of patients for the week ahead. There were so many emergencies today. A man around the age of 60 had a heart attack, but he's alright

now. My legs are really aching, after running around the hospital chasing a boy, who thinks its funny bursting into patients' rooms.
I suppose the last three days haven't been very interesting but that's just the life of a doctor.

Aswathi Nair (12)
Langdon School, London

A Day In The Life Of An Iraqi Soldier

After last night's attack, my city Baghdad was left looking like a junkyard. I could see buildings collapsed, it was like a smaller version of the September 11th attack. I could taste the dust flying about in the air. The smell of blood was rushing up into my nose, it smelt like a slaughterhouse.

In my mind all I could think about, was how my father died in the Gulf War. However, I bet my mother, at home, is praying for me. My little sister also crosses my mind all the time. I always look forward to seeing her after work.

As I start my first battle, fear is shivering down my spine. The sandstorms in the desert slow us down. Suddenly in the distance I see a little boy. I go to him and he asks me in a soft and broken voice for water. I give him some water and he says, 'Thank you. I am an orphan and I lost my family in last night's attack.'
I asked him where he was heading to. He gave no answer but then cried, 'Please take me with you.'
I left without answering him as I had to go when my captain called for me.

When I reached the captain he gave me a telegram. In the telegram it said that my family had been killed in last night's attack. I thought to myself, *why does there have to be war? Why can't there be peace in the world?*

Dulal Rahman (14)
Langdon School, London

THE FINAL MISTAKE

I stepped back, all the pressure was on me, to win the Interschool Cup over our rivals Leighton High. It would be our greatest feat ever.
'Come on Jonesy! You can do it,' screamed our goalie, whose nickname was Gobstopper.

Everybody called me by my surname, Jones; I can understand that, because my first name is Nardiello. I was bullied when I was smaller because of my name. But wait, why am I thinking about all this when I have to take the greatest kick in our school history?
'What side eh, left or right?'

Their goalie was trying to put me off. I took a deep breath and then the referee blew his whistle. I ran up and side-footed it, it was going in. I jumped and was in mid-air when a white hand flew and palmed it away.
'*Nooo*!' I shouted in disappointment.

The ref blew his whistle and called the two captains over. I bet he was going to rub the victory in our face, since he hated us. I saw them talking, he was going to award the cup at any moment, but then our captain jumped up and started screaming.
'We've won!' he was ecstatic.

I managed to calm him down and ask him what happened. He said the goalkeeper wasn't on his line when the penalty was taken so the win was given to us. In the end it was an anticlimax, but hey, we won the cup, that's all that matters. It also proved that cheats never win.

Jeevan Jyothyprakash (13)
Langdon School, London

THE HAUNTED HOUSE

Sarah threw the ball high up into the air, but Steph missed. The ball fell into an old, creepy, abandoned house with big iron gates.
'Go on, get the ball!' said Sarah.
'Me? Why should I get it? You're the one who threw it,' protested Steph.
'OK we'll go in together and get it,' said Sarah.

They both opened the big, iron gate and a loud creaking noise came. The two girls slowly walked towards the door. When they reached there, Sarah knocked on the door, using the rusty door knocker. The door opened but no one was there.

Inside, there was a massive staircase which spiralled towards the ceiling. There were cobwebs everywhere and a musty smell in the dark house.
'Umm, can we go now? That ball isn't worth going in there for,' said Steph, shaking.
'We've got this far, we can't back out now,' said Sarah, bravely.

They crept up the stairs, every step creaked as they went up. It seemed like the paintings on the walls were watching them. The eyes followed their every move. Even Sarah began to regret going in there, but the ball was just ahead of them. They could grab it and run. Steph picked the ball up and blew the dust off it.

Suddenly a big, furry, brown rat ran across Sarah's feet. They screamed and ran downstairs. Sarah opened the door and they ran outside the iron gates.

Sarah and Steph looked back at the house and saw something very strange. The house was surrounded by an unusual green glow. All of a sudden the house disappeared into thin air. Disappeared without leaving a trace.

Raeesa Kaiser (12)
Langdon School, London

GUN GANG TIE UP AND ROB TERRIFIED FAMILY!

A family needed hospital treatment after an armed gang broke into their home, tied them up and robbed their jewellery business.

The four robbers, following a carefully laid plan, forced their way into the house in East Ham at 4.30am on Wednesday. The robbers tied up the mother and her three children. They took the father to the jewellery store.

At the jewellery store the robbers cleared the shop of ten thousand pounds worth of jewellery. After stealing the jewellery, the robbers tied the father in the store and they left.

The family was able to free themselves about an hour and a half later and then called the police. Four members of the family had to go to hospital to be treated after they had minor injuries and were in shock.

'No CCTVs were on at the time of the robbery', said Inspector Keith. Which means there is no evidence.

Gurminderjit Boparai (12)
Langdon School, London

THE CURSE OF THE GOLDEN STATUE SNAKE

There is a curse, it may be true, it may be false. I am the person who's got this curse and now I am warning you, *do not touch the golden statue snake.*

It starts in ancient Aztec times when kings and queens used to rule. One day Mother told me to get some food to eat from the market. When I was going on my way I was thinking about the tax money we owed for the last few days. I was thinking where should I get it from.

When I was in the market, one old man told me that there was a reward for getting the golden statue snake. I asked the man what was the reward and he said that it was a room full of money. I was thinking that I could get the money to pay off tax. The man told me that the statue was in the temple of Inkara. I asked him where the temple was and he told me that it was in northern Mexico.

I bought some food and started to walk home. All the way I was thinking whether I should do it or not.

When I got home, my mother and I sat down to eat. Mother was telling me about the tax and I told her that I would get the money by tonight.

I went to get the statue snake from the temple. I got to the temple by donkey and it took me half a day to get there. When I finally arrived I started digging near the temple. I was trying to dig underneath but in the hole that I dug, hundreds of snakes came out, so that way was blocked to me.

I tired to break down the temple's walls with a heavy wooden log. That did work but there were snakes there as well. I had no choice but to step on the snakes and go to get the statue snake.

When I saw the statue there were snakes, millions of them. I just ran on top of the snakes to get the statue. When I grabbed it my hands and face turned into reptile skin. My eyes started to turn green and I started to get smaller and more flexible. Before I knew it I had turned into a snake.

Now I know that the snakes on the floor were people who were trying to get the golden statue snake!

Muneer Patel (13)
Langdon School, London

THE DECEMBER 2002 RED ALERT!

December 2002 was one of the most exciting months in Premiership history! The 'big three' of Arsenal, Liverpool and Manchester United were all playing each other in a mouth-watering series of matches, and whoever was to come out on top would look forward to a very prosperous New Year.

A look at the history books reveals some interesting statistics. The 10 Premiership matches between Liverpool and Manchester United at Anfield, both sides achieved a massive 36 goals.

With Owen, Diouf, Heskey, Barras, van Nistelrooy, Giggs and Solskjaer all expected to feature at some point, the pattern looked as though it was set to continue.

Six days later Manchester United welcomed Arsenal to Old Trafford. The Londoners have only lost one in five seasons at the Theatre Of Dreams, but there was that one game a 6-1 thrashing by an inspired United in February in 2001 it has now become a part of Old Trafford legend.

Four days after Christmas it was the turn of Liverpool to head to London to defend their excellent Highbury record. Liverpool had won five times there since the introduction of the Premiership. There were records to extend and plenty of points to be won for the three reds, as the Premiership season was reaching a critical stage.

After waiting through the worrying and deciding matches, the points were added up to conclude Arsenal had won the December 2002 Premiership. It was a very happy moment for Arsenal as they had won and at the same time celebrating the New Year with some very high hopes for 2003!

Jasmin Bansal (13)
Langdon School, London

HEADACHE

Once, there was a little boy who was asleep. This little boy was not very responsible. He forgot a lot of important things like his homework. Sometimes he would start a piece of homework, decide to play his computer for a while, get carried away, and end up leaving his homework till late. Other times, he would forget about the homework completely! But sometimes he sincerely couldn't do it.

This time he had forgotten his English homework. He woke up the next day and the first thought that came to his head was, *Aw nuts, I forgot my English homework! There's no way I can go to school today.*
'Mum, I've got a headache.'
'Have your breakfast then talk to me about headaches,' said his mum, seeing right through his little scheme and expected him to forget about it after breakfast.

He ate his breakfast and then his friends came to go with him to school. Then he remembered about his headache. 'Mum, I've still got a headache.'
Assuming he was telling the truth, because he remembered, his mum let him stay at home.

When his mum left for work, he started playing on his computer. He completely forgot about his homework again. He went to bed very happily that night. But the next day . . .
'Mum, I've got a headache!'

Jermaine Anderson (13)
Langdon School, London

How The Hare And The Tortoise Became Friends

Long ago, in a faraway land there lived a hare and a tortoise. The hare would always tease the tortoise about how slow the tortoise walked and the tortoise would always get upset.

One day, at the animal academy, as usual the tortoise and his friends were having a race when along came the hare.
'Well, well, what do we have here? Slow coach running!' said the hare. 'No matter how hard he tries he will never win.'

The tortoise became angry. He always had to listen to the hare's nasty comments and wasn't going to take it any longer.
'If you're so sure that I can't win, why don't you prove it?' he screamed in anger.
'Fine! You and me will race at noon next week. The race will start at the apple tree and end at the river.' The hare and his friends walked off.

'How on earth will I ever be able to win against the hare? He runs so much faster than I do,' said the anxious tortoise.
'Don't worry, we'll think of something,' assured Tortoise's friends.

The day of the race soon came and Tortoise was nervous.
'Don't worry. We've got it all under control. When the hare is not looking, one of us will put this sleeping tablet in his drink. He will fall fast asleep while you will reach the finishing line,' said the tortoise's friends.

The race started. After a while the hare started to feel sleepy. He went and sat in the shade of a tree and feel fast asleep. Meanwhile, the tortoise had reached the finishing line. The tortoise's friends cheered him while the other animals were amazed. The hare was nowhere to be seen. The tortoise and his friends went looking for the hare.

'Help!' shouted a voice. It was coming from the edge of the cliff. The tortoise walked over there to find the hare hanging from a branch. The tortoise and his friends helped the hare up.

'I must have been sleep walking again. Thank you for saving my life. I'll never tease you, ever again. Friends?' said the hare with relief. 'Friends,' said the tortoise and they were friends forever after.

Janki Vaghela (13)
Langdon School, London

The Restless Noise

After just having said goodnight to my parents I went to bed. This was my first night in my new house, we had just moved in today.

I was fast asleep when I was awakened by loud banging noises. I tried my best to ignore them but it was impossible. The noise was coming from the ceiling as if something was trying to make a hole in it.

The noise grew louder and louder. I heard dogs barking as if they were dying a long, agonising death. The branches of the tree outside were banging on the window. The room felt like it was moving all around me. I clung onto the mattress with all my strength. I peered outside the window and saw a shadow brush past. I was as cold as ice and as white as snow. I glanced at the window one last time and could see the light from the sun gently rising above the mountains in the far distance. At that precise moment the noise stopped.

The next day at school I was learning about Egyptians and that rumours said that in the year 2003, mummies would come alive to kill anyone who lived in their area.

When I got home my mum told me to ignore all that nonsense. She said, 'This house was said to be an ancient Egyptian burial place for cats . . . I haven't heard or seen anything strange.'
'But!'
'No buts, now get to bed.'

I was awakened by all the noises coming from the attic and this time I decided to investigate. I climbed up the stairs, turned the handle to the attic door and proceeded up.

It was very dark and therefore I grabbed a flashlight. I was in pure shock for what I saw beyond me was an Egyptian cat. I dropped the flashlight on the floor and at that moment the cat seized me and pulled me in the air. I reached for the flashlight and shone it into the centre of his eyes. This must have blinded him because he flew back and hit his head on the shelf which had an old glass of water on it, which fell on his head. Just then I remembered that cats hate water, so I took the opportunity and grabbed an old spit bucket, which was beside me and threw it onto the cat. The cat began to disintegrate into the water.

I shut my eyes for just a second and when I opened them I was somehow in my bed half asleep. *At least I can sleep in peace now,* I thought to myself and I just shut my eyes.

Ashley Davis (12)
Langdon School, London

NATASHA AND TOBY

Who was the fool that said two people born at the same time, under the same array of stars would be alike? Natasha and Toby were born within moment of each other - and to the same mother - but there were never two humans more different. Everything about Natasha was beautiful, from the smooth insides of her wrists to the colours in her dreams. Everything about Toby was ugly, from his acid yellow eyes to the mischief he kept in his heart.

When they were born, there was little more to the world than pine trees and a sprinkling of stars overhead. Natasha looked around her and wondered how she could make life easier for the people and animals living there, so she created flat, sunny meadows, sweetcorn and maple syrup, medicinal herbs and moose hide, spring, holidays, apple trees and fur coats for the bears.

Toby, on the other hand, looked around him and wondered what he could do to make life more difficult. He created cacti and leeches, poisonous berries and rattlesnakes, cliffs, deserts, witchcraft, sorcery and Monday mornings.

The worst of all his mischief, he saved for his sister. Toby longed to kill Natasha. Though they had been born to live for several thousand years, Toby knew there was a way of killing her, if only he could discover the secret.

'I have to admit,' he said one day, 'I've been mortally afraid of ferns ever since Mother told me that the fern root would be the death of me.' Then he smiled a sickly smile. 'Surely nothing could kill you, though, Dear sister? Not the glorious Natasha?'
'It's owl feathers with me,' said Natasha and she marvelled at the speed with which her brother hurried away.

Toby went at once and found his bow. At dusk, he shot an owl out of a tree and wrenched a bunch of feathers out of its limp little body. Creeping up behind his sister, he broke the feather over her head. Instantly Natasha fell dead.

Toby stood holding the drooping feather, his jaw hanging open in delight, his tongue dangling. It had been so easy! Now he was the lord of all nature. First to make absolutely sure Natasha was dead, Toby slunk closer. The hands were still and the eyelids did not flicker. He would just hold his cheek close to the lips, to feel for signs of breathing . . .

As he did so Natasha sneezed directly down his ear, yawned and sat up. Although she was gentle and peaceable, Natasha was far from stupid.
'I said an owl's feather would kill me. I didn't say anything about staying dead,' she pointed out.

Toby's face went red while he tried to hide the owl feathers in his pocket.

Wasif Saeed Sheikh (13)
Langdon School, London

A Day In The Life Of A Secret Spy

Monday 27th April

I bolted out of bed with a start, there was gossip in the air. I just knew it. I could tell by the smell of the outdoors and by also by the way the morning birds twittered. I also knew I was late for school.

I ran down the stairs in such a hurry, I could have been described as a Mexican tornado. In a matter of minutes I was somewhat decent and seeing as I had a few seconds to spare, I made myself a quick sarnie.

After I had finished doing that, I left home and went to the bus stop to catch a bus. I brought my notebook along with me to jot down anything peculiar. When the bus finally arrived, I tried to find a free seat next to the window but I couldn't, so I stood up and observed the other passengers.

I happened to notice a rather queer-looking man, whose right hand was constantly tapping at his trouser pocket, almost as if there was something valuable inside it. I tried to look even closer and I saw what seemed to be the outline of a gun.

I was stricken with panic and I was in two different minds, should I alert the other passengers and risk getting killed or stay quiet and see what happened.

No one said being a spy was easy work and sometimes you need to take a few risks but you also need to be 100% certain and I wasn't.

I tried to take the easy way out and was about to get off at the next stop when I realised that the doors were stuck. I was trapped, it was like I'd been taken hostage.

The bus driver had an evil glint in his eye. From now on I will trust no one. There is nothing else to do other than hope and pray.

May Sulaiman (13)
Langdon School, London

THE DAY IN THE LIFE OF LANGDON'S SCHOOL ROUNDABOUT

School starting - students start arriving . . . 8.55am and students (late) start arriving. All this chatter, laughing and shouting is so predictable, it's the same conversations every day!
'Oh my daze! They said that . . . I wouldn't take . . .'
'Damn! I forgot my homework!'
'Pass it . . . pass it!'
'Look at my new boots . . . looking good init!'
Don't these students talk about anything else . . .

Lunchtime.
The smell of the food is intoxicating me, it's all the same smell - hot dogs, kebabs, chips, pizza etc. When will these students ever have healthy food . . . It's 1.20pm and students are rushing back.

After school.
The whole of the school is standing on me, what's so interesting? I can't see anything! A teacher shouts, the crowd cheers! There, I see two students, both bleeding, both ready to knock each other out. However, then I see another student on the floor, blood pouring out of his head . . . I know this boy . . . he's got a reputation of being a racist. Wonders never cease to amaze me. Nothing shocks me anymore . . . fights, fireworks, eggings, expulsion walks, waterfights, jokes, joyriders, tears, trips and tantrums, I've seen, I've heard them all. It's nothing new, but it's the roundabout for Langdon school . . . what else is there to expect?

Aliya Malik (13)
Langdon School, London

ENGRAVINGS

Some people have gas fires. Not us. We have a big stone fireplace. I wish we had a gas fire. A small, ugly, inefficient gas fire. What would a gas fire remind you of? The flaming thumb advert for British Gas. I wouldn't mind that. But our fireplace . . . it has engravings. Every time something eventful happens, we engrave the fireplace. There's my name and the date of my birth. The day Mum and Dad got married. The day I took my first steps, the day I talked, the day I cut my first tooth, my first day at school. The day Dad died.

I remember it so clearly. Dad had been ill for a while, but I never imagined it was that serious. He was at home for God's sake! So one day I woke up, kissed Mum and Dad goodbye and I walked to school. It was a good day. We were studying Ancient Romans in history. I didn't even get a sense of foreboding, not even when I got right near the house.

I opened the door very quietly. I didn't want to wake Dad up. I could hear crying. That's when I knew, I just knew something had happened. I tiptoed quietly, quietly into the living room. Mum was there. She was holding the special knife we use for engravings. I could see what she had written: 'James Le Breton, 1958-2003'. He was dead. My father was dead. That was the day I went numb.

Catie Le Prevost (15)
Les Beaucamps Secondary School, Guernsey

THE KISS

I wake to a horse-marathon. The million hooves on the roof, across the chimney top. I stare at the scene of the cloud-pearls tumbling through air, hurtling at the crystal glass, jumping the distance from the snow-black roof to the ground, like lemmings. The scene seems oddly reckless to me now . . . the reason hits, as my face freezes.

I stretch out for the water to stop the desert spreading in my mouth. Scowling at my cereal, I dared it to make a move, or to tell my thoughts to anybody in particular.
'Thomas . . .'
Running out of time . . . I reach for my glass.

I stroll across the playground on hot coals. I'm determined to get it right. There she is! No, no, no, no!

I watch her with lemon in my eyes, as she leaves crushed ice in her footsteps, roasts strangers with a glance. I grin, a fool, and in return her black magic smile. My eyes rush towards her. The slightest, coincidental, torturing touch was *it*.

My hands, despite the screaming warning in my head, fight their way through the woodsmoke air. 'Billie?'
She turns her icicle eyes and I shiver. We stare at each other, two melting snowmen. I gently press the faint wisp of scarlet hair behind her ear, frozen in heat.

And it happens: a firecracker kiss. I close my eyes. My mind numbs, leaving only that blissful buzz and the taste of liquorice on fire.

The horses race down my spine.

Thomas Lynam (16)
Ludlow CE School, Shropshire

Is This The End?

On April 8th 2003, something terrible happened at the football stadium in Madrid, the whole stadium caught fire and had to be closed down until further notice.

16-year-old James Star, 18-year-old Callum French, 23-year-old Daniel White and 27-year old Michael Bar, all from London, went to Madrid to see United play Madrid. They caused a huge riot when the match ended and the score was 3-1. All of the Madrid fans were cheering at the result of the game and the four rioters ran over to them, randomly attacking them by punching and kicking. The security caught 18-year-old Callum French, as he tripped over his bag and stumbled to the floor. As he was being lifted on his feet, he was struggling to get free, also he was shouting abusive language. At one point, James Star lit a match and threw it a couple of rows down. His friends did the same thing, the whole way around the stadium. Soon United fans were swarming in and hurling the lit matches everywhere.

Nobody got seriously hurt, but three people, Jack Williams aged 30, Thomas Green aged 8 and Bethany Walker aged 15, got burn scars because they were running around. Michael Bar was seen to open his rucksack and pull out a massive petrol can. He poured it over the fire and soon the stadium was blazing with flames at 30 metres high. Daniel White also got a petrol can out of his bag and was seen frantically splashing it about.

The police swarmed in from all directions and caught all of the rioters. Shortly after the fire brigade began spraying water for over two-and-a-half hours and managed to put the fire out.

The rioters were arrested and the four that started it pleaded guilty at Widbury police station. They are being dealt with severely and stadium builders reckon that in one year the stadium will be back to normal. Security say they are starting a new rule to let viewers into the stadium, but further notice will be reported.

Melissa Koekemoer (12)
Parklands High School, Manchester

A Few Days In The Life Of A Victorian Boy Called Billy

April 2nd 1837

Today, my revolting boss sent me up another stinking chimney. But this one was different. It was steep and had about thirty sharp and curvy bends. It was grubby, full of thick dust and soot. I nearly got stuck! I thought to myself, *why should I put up with this?* It should be stopped. Kids like me should be able to play and be educated at school. Maybe we can actually achieve something in life. Oh well, tomorrow is another day.

April 3rd 1837

I got the sack today! Hooray! No more slavery, no more being pushed around and especially no more chimneys. Now with my saved wages, I can go shopping and buy a new diary and a new pen. I must be the luckiest boy alive, I think!

May 14th 1837

Yesterday, after my reunion with Mum, I signed up at the local school. When I skipped to the shabby building, I noticed one of my friends, Harry. He was being tortured and whipped because he'd refused to go up a chimney on his own. I bellowed at the man. He let go and Harry ran off. I was relieved he was safe now. But the man came storming over to me. So, quick as a flash, I galloped to school.

My day there was unbelievably fascinating.

Kelsey Easton (12)
Parklands High School, Manchester

TWO DAYS IN THE LIFE OF A SOLDIER

March 20th 2003

Dear Diary,

In less than 19 minutes we're going to war on Saddam Hussein. We've been trying to catch him for the last 12 years, but have not yet succeeded.

He possesses mass destruction nuclear bombs, as well as chemical bombs. This is one of the main reasons we're going to war, because he won't destroy them.

I am missing my wife and children already, and we've only been gone five days. This sounds really ridiculous, because we could be at war for months. The army promises that it will be over as quickly as possible.

I can't bare to think how many innocent lives will be lost, such as Iraqi civilians, British and American soldiers.

We have been told that England and America are a high risk for terrorist attacks.

March 25th 2003

Dear Diary,

We are now officially at war with Iraq. Many of the Iraqi soldiers have surrendered. Over the last five nights we have dropped at least 20 bombs on Saddam's secret hideouts, over Baghdad.

No one has yet seen Saddam. He has appeared on Iraqi TV a few times, but we don't know if it is him, because he has so many lookalikes.

Two nights ago we almost caught him, but there have been rumours that he's planning to make an appearance on TV to prove that he and his sons are perfectly fine.

We all know that Saddam Hussein is an evil man, who deserves to be prosecuted or dead.

Sergeant Whitby.

Aviva Nelson (12)
Parklands High School, Manchester

TIGER ON THE RUN!

I was sat at home watching the TV when suddenly a newsflash came on saying that a white tiger was running wild! The tiger had got out from the zoo, right near my house. The woman on the news said to cover up our windows and lock our doors. So I covered the windows and locked the door, hoping the tiger would not come to my door.

I started to watch the TV again, I didn't hear of the tiger for the rest of the night. Until the morning.

I turned on the TV to see if anything had gone on. A newsflash was on. The white tiger was right next to my house, he was on the green, I just sat there. I was very scared. I just sat on the sofa, trying not to think of the white tiger on the green.

I went upstairs to have a nap, when all of a sudden I hear a big bang! I went downstairs slowly, trying to see what had happened. There it was, eating all the cat food, a great, big, hairy, white and black . . . cat. It just sat there. All this time people thought it was a white tiger, when really it was just a white cat wanting food.

Jessica Gibson (12)
Parklands High School, Manchester

A Day In The Life Of An Iraqi Civilian

I was forced out of bed at 5am by the soldiers. I didn't get much sleep over the noise of bombs. The whole of my area was unbelievable and wrecked.

I received some water by the humanitarian group, I felt so thirsty before they came. Then I went to school and our tutor told us that if a bomb went off, we weren't to panic. A bomb did go off later that day, it scared me and my friends to death . . . it really did! Both of my parents died in front of my very eyes. It was so unbearable.

Later that day, I was collected by a helicopter and while I was in it, my back had an awful pain - that's all I could remember.

The next day I woke up with an humanitarian aid member next to me. He said that we couldn't travel abroad, as Baghdad's airport had been badly bombed.

It's now half-past six and I'm on my sheet and pillow. I wish Iraq was back to normal and . . . oh no . . . ! a soldier's coming to get me . . . !

Lacey Holden (12)
Parklands High School, Manchester

THE EARTH WILL SHAKE AGAIN!

Last night the whole of England was shaken by a massive earthquake. It only lasted for a minute, but caravans got knocked over, chimney pots fell of the top of houses and roads cracked in two.

One person, Joanne from Manchester, was on her way home from work when it struck. She said, 'It was awful. Cars were sliding everywhere and people were running and screaming. Some people even got buried in the ruins of buildings'.

Over 800,000 people in England got injured last night and over 2,000 are dead. The hospitals are full of people waiting to be seen.

Just for one minute, this earthquake has done untold damage to a lot of people in England. All the schools are now closed and doctors and nurses still want to go to work, even though they are injured. Shops, factories and work places are now closed, maybe for a week.

Although children are not in school, they are not very happy as they think there may be a lot more earthquakes. Some will not be as bad as the one last night, but some may be worse.

The earthquake that struck last night, was the worst in 35 years. News reporters are telling everyone to be aware and to stock up on food.

Emma McMenamin (12)
Parklands High School, Manchester

IT'S RAINING CATS AND DOGS

It's raining cats and dogs - literally. Meteorologists cannot explain this weird weather. People are confused as to why Jack Russells and Persian cats are dropping out of the sky.

We asked a few people about their opinions: Mrs Madam - 'My son thinks it's great, he's always wanted a puppy, however my opinion is different, mainly because they put a dint in your umbrella'.

Mr Sir - 'I can't walk into the street without a Jack Russell nipping at my ankle or a cat scratching me, I've been through five suits today already'.

Mad Scientist - 'I'm afraid that the Earth's ground is sinking. We're going to have to move to another planet and the cat and dog droppings stink'.

God - 'I didn't do it, don't blame me. It wasn't my fault. For once I didn't cause the problem. Why don't you go and ask another god, Anubis or someone?' Well, if God didn't do it, who did? Maybe the Queen, maybe the boy with holes in his socks? We may never know. My question is, why Jack Russells and not German shepherds or maybe even a Golden Retriever? Who's going to stop this very weird weather?

More reports on the weather tomorrow, there will also be more from me.

Scott Wilkinson (11)
Parklands High School, Manchester

A Few Days In The Life Of A Dog Called Billy

June 16th

I don't know where I am, a big man took me away with a little girl. She picked me up and ran out of my home with me, leaving without my mum. At first I was there with her and then I was sat somewhere very smelly. I started to cry because it all happened so fast, but it was really silly of me to do so. The big man came out whistling, putting something into his back pocket. I got frightened and curled up.

June 30th

I don't actually like that girl anymore. She keeps standing on my feet and pulling my tail, on purpose! I've cried at the washroom door for over five days now, when they say it's time for bed, but the thing is, I can still hear them watching the TV. They turn the light out so it's really dark, then scream at me until I go to the cardboard box they call my bed!

July 17th

I'm bigger now and I'm getting stronger teeth. I bit that girl the other day, boy did she scream! I just ran into the other room like nothing at all had happened. That man as well, he keeps going on at me just 'cause I had a bit of a smelly accident on his work shoes. 'It'll come off, but just leave a brown mark!' I barked.

I'm thinking of running away. No one likes me here.

Shauna Summers (12)
Parklands High School, Manchester

THE MAD BOMBER STRIKES AGAIN!

Today, the so-called 'Mad Bomber' has struck again! This time he targeted Manchester's Arndale centre.

Police believe that a 10,000lb bomb was planted in 'The Cut Above Creations' barber shop. Over 3,000 victims of this horrific crime, were killed. 100 passers-by were seriously injured and needed immediate medical attention and around 25 civilians were slightly burnt.

An on the scene reporter, shooting a fashion show opposite, stated, 'It was absolutely terrible. The smell of smoke blocked my lungs. The impact of the explosion caused every pane of glass to fly out of the windows'.

The Mad Bomber has struck three times in the last month! The police are looking for witnesses who may know anything at all about this terrorist. Chief Inspector Davies gave an explicit warning, directly to the bomber on international television. He said, 'I cannot emphasise how much I want you to come forward. I want to contact you in any way I can. I want to know why you are doing this. Please stop now! This has gone far enough, thousands of innocent people have been killed. Stop now! Think about what you are doing!'

This speech shocked the viewing world and touched the hearts of millions of people. As a token of sorrow, many of the funerals, for the people who died today, are being paid for by the Government.

Andrew Taylor (12)
Parklands High School, Manchester

DAYS IN THE LIFE OF A SOLDIER

Day 1 - It's my first day today and training is hard, though satisfying to know it's for a good cause.

Day 2 - I'm missing my family, I know my wife Natasha could have our baby anytime now! My new car is due tomorrow and I wish I'd never volunteered now!

Day 4 - Blair is now having conferences and we are watching and waiting to see if we are going to war. I should be at home, watching this with my wife.

Day 7 - War! It has been declared and I am flying our to Iraq in two days. I wish I could have a chance to say goodbye to my family.

Day 8 - I have just phoned home and, and . . .

Day 9 - I'm in the back of an F15 fighter jet, just crossing Ireland. I am having second thoughts now . . .

Day 10 - We're now shooting. I don't think I've killed anyone yet, but time will tell.

Day 11 - I know for definite that I have just killed an innocent Iraqi. I can't pick up the gun, *'Help!'*

Day 15 - My best friend John, has been killed in friendly fire. I feel like shouting to the Heavens, 'Let's kick some Iraqi butt!'

Day 22 - We're moving into Baghdad and . . .

Alex was killed on day 22. His diary was found after the war.

Alex Hickson (12)
Parklands High School, Manchester

SADDAM IS DROPPED

'War is almost over', say the Americans. Hundreds of Iraqis are flocking the streets to celebrate their freedom from Saddam Hussein's regime. In the centre of Iraq today, people came to watch the statue of Saddam Hussein being pulled to the ground, in a symbolic act against his oppressive regime.

Working together, US Marines helped crowds of Iraqi men bring down the imposing monument. On the day, Baghdad's population celebrated its liberation with pride.

In scenes reminiscent of the fall of the Berlin Wall, civilians worked with the troops, to attach a noose around the statue's neck in the city square.

These scenes of celebration spread later, to Arbil in Northern Iraq, where crowds have gathered to celebrate their freedom and their joy of not having Saddam Hussein as their leader. Iraqis were celebrating in rather odd ways. Men were getting their slippers and hitting pictures of Saddam Hussein. As the American troops travelled through Baghdad, Iraqi men were cheering and whistling to say thank you.

After pulling down the statue, men were dancing on and around the collapsed monument. There are also still searches for Saddam in the rubble left of the mansion, that once belonged to him and his sons.

Soldiers will continue the search for Saddam and will track his sons down. Then the Iraqis can live in peace and hope for a better leader to help them.

Rachel Porritt (12)
Parklands High School, Manchester

THE HIDDEN FIFTH

His deep blue eyes searched her green ones, as she struggled to undo herself from his tight grasp. His face moved forever towards hers, and their lips entwined in a breathless kiss, as his hands stroked the back of her neck. She tried to break free of his kiss, but he tightened the grip on her neck. She was struggling to breathe and now both of his hands were around her neck. She gagged, tried to call his name. The kiss had finished and his grip was slowly tightening. He whispered in her ear that he loved her, as she took her final breath. He released her and her lifeless body slumped to the ground. He took one final look at her and turned and walked calmly away, her motionless body not affecting him in any way. 'One down, three to go,' he muttered to himself.

The young girl smiled at his comments, and she stared into his deep blue eyes. He leaned in to kiss her, and after a second he broke it off. 'I have a present for you!' he whispered. He produced a gold necklace and handed it to her. Then he took it back and placed it round her neck. She was laughing out loud; she couldn't remember the last time she had felt so happy, so full of life. He fumbled with the clasp and when it was done, he put his hands around her neck and tightened them. She tried to move his hands, but his grip was too tight. 'I love you,' he whispered again, as she took her final gasp of the polluted city air. His grip tightened and she went limp in his hands. Her feeling of being so full of life had shattered into a thousand pieces, containing a hundred times more bad luck than a broken mirror. He turned and left, nonchalantly lighting a cigarette as he went.

The third was more difficult to charm, he even thought the fourth would be simple. She was resisting his charm, playing hard to get. But she'd come round. They all did . . . however long it took, he'd wait.

He'd got her. He knew he would. She'd trusted him, allowed him to get a bit closer than he should, being her brother-in-law. But now she was gone. Strangled by his own bare hands. He'd asked her to meet him in an abandoned alleyway . . . he still couldn't work out why she'd agreed. Nonetheless, she'd come. He'd turned around to tie his shoelace and when he stood up, his hands had found their way to her neck. The last words she heard were, 'I'm sorry,' as her still-warm body slid to the dirty pavement below. He blew her a kiss and silently asked for forgiveness.

She laughed at his words, the feeling of his hands running of her skin. He stroked her stomach, large as she was, seven months pregnant, his wife. He kissed her hand, her arm, her neck and finally her lips and his hands stroked her hair. His hands moved down her hair towards her neck. His grasp tightened around her neck, strong but slow. This had to be a slow, painful death. He was muttering in her ear sorries and messages of love. She thrashed about, trying to release herself. She couldn't work out how things could have gone from kisses to strangulation. She took her last look at the world, had her last thought, heard her last sound, took her last breath. Her unresponsive body slumped onto her cream carpet.

The man looked at her and laughed. The fourth girl was gone. The first boy . . . the hidden fifth . . . was also gone. He cared nothing, felt no remorse, cared nothing for the innocent lives lost at his guilt-ridden hands. No soul existed in his cold, callous body.

One foot following the other, his cruel, pitiful mind commanded him to walk out of his door, into the street and out into the bustling city centre. As he mingled with the gullible crowd, he prepared himself for his next challenge . . . police . . . ghosts . . . Jimminy Crickett . . .

Kirsty Cable (15)
Pierowall Junior High School, Orkney

A Day In The Life Of Annie Brooks, Aged 12 . . .

1st January

Dear Diary,

This is an important day for me because today is the day that I start my new job. It will be at the factory a mile away. It is 6am, I am fairly tired but I'll survive.

One hour later . . .

I have now reached the factory, it is fairly large, that explains the fact of why it was so busy. I felt like a needle in a haystack. So lonely and afraid. I didn't know anybody. My mouth was dry, and just to put the icing on the cake, a large man came and stood right in front of me. I figured he was the manager. He then stared at me, he then told me to start walking so I did. He showed me to my work area and then informed me that if I had any major problems, I'd just have to tell him.

2nd January

Dear Diary,

This time I got up earlier just to impress. Today would probably be easier, considering the hardest part was over. I started work straight away. Today he said I'd be working with the machines. I obviously got straight to work. I was started to fit in and I felt more involved.

A few weeks later . . .

Dear Diary,

Everything has been going great until now; you see something terrible has happened. My friend had an accident with the machine and unfortunately she is badly injured. They're not sure if she will survive.

A few days later . . .

Dear Diary,

Luckily I got some information from her. She is alright.

Night, night Diary.

Amy Yates (12)
Pool Hayes Community School, West Midlands

THE DRAGON CHAMPION

Long ago when dragons roamed free across the land, there lived an evil wizard called the Thunder Demon. He was a horrible man who would control the dragons and use them to get what he wanted, but all that would soon change.

Marmoth was an adventurous man who loved horse riding but always had a fascination for dragons. He was once bitten by a dragon and had had a strange feeling inside ever since and now it suddenly it had awakened. He was Marmoth the dragon champion.

He knew that someone was controlling the dragons. He could feel it in his veins and in his blood. So he called his trusty dragon friend, the strongest of all, Crimson.

As they flew into the pitch-black night sky, not knowing where they were going, they saw an enormous flash of purple light. It was the Thunder Demon. As he swooped down towards them, there was a giant explosion. Suddenly their was a giant earthquake that knocked the Thunder Demon off balance and he was on the ground.
'Prepare to die!' said Marmoth.
'No, you can't kill me!'
'Why?' said Marmoth.
'Because . . . I'll ask nicely.'
'Go on then!' said Marmoth.
'. . .No I can't do it!'
'Well then die!'
With that final blow the Thunder Demon was dead. A fantastic shot, right between the eyes.

With the death of the Thunder Demon, Marmoth and the rest of the dragons lived happily ever after.

Steven Morris (12)
Pool Hayes Community School, West Midlands

A BUMFACE STORY JUST FOR GOLD

The pirate Bumface, was the leader of other pirates. He was looking for gold. There was another pirate called One-Eyed Pete who was the leader of another band of pirates. One-Eyed Pete was after the gold as well.

When Bumface was on an island resting, one of his pirates had spied a rope in some trees and Bumface decided to make it into a swing. The pirates needed some wood for a stand for the swing and they all went searching for wood. All of the time the wood was right in front of them - the trees! They started cutting down the trees and as they did they heard a loud *bang!*

They left the cover of the trees and they saw a big black ship and on it was One-Eyed Pete. Bumface and all his shipmates got on board their ship and got ready to fire on the black ship.

Bumface told them when to fire. One of the other ship's shots hit them but they had five hits on the black ship and it began to sink.

'I'll get you!' shouted One-Eyed Pete but it was too late and he and all his men drowned.

There were no more worries about Bumface getting the gold and when he did he spent it on all kinds of things for himself and his shipmates.

Sarah Whitehouse (12)
Pool Hayes Community School, West Midlands

THE FIRST DANGER

Up at the top of Mount Snowmore there lived a yeti. The yeti was white and had two heads. The head on the left was called Ray and the other was called Einstein. With their pet snow dragon Avalanche, they destroyed all the people of Mata Nui who tried to climb Mount Snowmore. They would cover Mata Nui with a blanket of snow.

As the Yeti and his pet destroyed everything the people of Mata Nui were getting angry, they wanted to kill the yeti but none of them were strong enough to do it. So Ray and Einstein carried on with their destruction.

One day a man came flying on a blue-eyed, white dragon called Arthur. The man swore he would vanquish the yeti. So he and Arthur began to climb up Mount Snowmore.

After a long climb, they came face to face with the yeti. The man told the beast to leave the mountain and never come back. But the beast refused. The man warned him that if he didn't leave he would destroy the yeti. It would have to fight the beast. After a long battle the man destroyed the beast.

Suddenly, a cave emerged from the snow. As he entered the cave he realised that the cave was a lot warmer than outside. As he went deeper into the cave he saw an inscription on the wall which read, *The yeti of Mount Snowmore is just the first danger. The defeater of the yeti marks the coming of the Borok swarms and the destruction of Mata Nui.*

Suddenly the ground shook and six pillars arose. The man could hear someone or something talking in a strange language to someone else. Then it all went quiet . . .

Greg Corbett (11)
Pool Hayes Community School, West Midlands

THE LORD OF DRAGONS

One day there lived a young boy from the black lands. He got separated from his parents while they were walking. While the boy was searching for his mother and father he came across an injured dragon.

The boy approached the dragon very slowly. He touched its wound but instead of feeling pain the wound started to heal. Over the next few days his mother and father had lost hope. The dragon had taken the boy to his lair where he and the other dragons lived in harmony. The boy stayed there until he was an adult. He had heard that the evil winged-dragon was coming to terrorise the dragon's lair.

Our hero stepped up to the dragon and scared it. He was known to the winged-dragons as a menace and had to be destroyed. They swore that they would return.

While our hero was treating a sick dragon, the winged-dragons were attacking! Our hero grabbed the first sharp thing he could and started hacking down all the evil dragons.

Eventually the battle was over. The mystic dragons had won and all the winged-dragons were destroyed. Nothing that was evil lived.

Our hero was now know as The Lord Of The Dragons.

Alex Faulkner (12)
Pool Hayes Community School, West Midlands

THE DIARY OF A GIRL CALLED CLARRISA

9th February 2003

Dear Diary

Nobody understands me. Today I was just trying to show some concern and my friend Macy told me to go away and said it was none of my business. But it is my business because I have been her friend for ages. She said that because I don't have anything like this happening to me, I poke my nose in, when it happens to be somebody else; yeah so I didn't get dumped by my last boyfriend but it isn't like I don't know what she's going through.

10th February 2003

Dear Diary

Macy still isn't talking to me, usually when we have arguments we are talking by the next day but this time we aren't. I think it's serious this time. Next time I see her I'm going to say that I'm sorry and I shouldn't have tried to give her something that she didn't want.

11th February 2003

Dear Diary

Well I told her and we made up but we didn't talk that much today. I think that she's still trying to work out what to do. I'm not saying anything, if she wants my help she'll ask for it.

12th February 2003

Dear Diary

She asked me for help with her problem today, so I helped her. She asked him out again and they got back together. I have never seen her so happy, I'm glad she asked him out again.

Jessie Edwards (12)
Pool Hayes Community School, West Midlands

THE SILVER KNIGHT AND THE CREATURE

There once was a knight who wore the most beautiful armour. It glowed in the dark, the colour of silver. He was one of the bravest knights.

One night, when it was quiet and dark, something crept carefully out that had been behind the bushes in the king's garden all day. A long slim body searched for food. Only a glimpse could be seen, leaving footprints as it left.

Soon morning came, 'Arrggh! Something has been here and left footprints,' the people shouted as they rushed around.
The silver knight was sent for by the king, 'Find the creature!' he demanded.

I'll try the woods first, thought the silver knight. He searched high and low but what he didn't know was that he was being followed. Suddenly he heard a noise, he slowly turned around and shouted, 'Arrggh!' He did get a fright but what was standing there was a small furry creature.
'Hello, who are you?' asked the creature.
'What are you?' asked the silver knight.
'I'm a fox,' said the creature.

The silver knight scooped the fox into his arms and soon they were at the castle. 'This creature will not harm you,' said the silver knight to the king. 'He lives in the wild and all he wants to do is look after his family.'

From that day on nobody ever worried about the foxes again. People would often take food to the woods for them. The silver knight would often visit the harmless foxes and the foxes lived a happy life.

Cally Staffiere (11)
Pool Hayes Community School, West Midlands

ONE DAY BEING TIGGER

Ooooo, that was a nice sleep. I love this chair, it's so comfy. I don't really want to move, but I can hear the human in the kitchen. There might be some food, so I suppose I'd better get up.

I can see her picking up the bowls so I guess she's putting the food out and into the bowls. I can smell my cat food, *mmm*. I jump over the back of the chair because I hear her call.
'Tig-Tig, Bash-Bash.'
I chew away and then after five minutes I'm gone, running outside.

Once I'm outside, I jump over next-door's fence and run into their dirt patch and start to roll about until my housemate comes along. It's Ash, up my paws go and we start to fight.

After two hours of adventures I come in and jump on the human's lap. The human starts to fuss me. *Purr, purr*, mmm, so sleepy . . .

Donna Russon (11)
Pool Hayes Community School, West Midlands

A Day In The Life Of Sabrina The Teenage Witch

1st April
Dear Diary,
Today I got up at 7.30am. I got washed and dressed and had my breakfast. At 8.15am, my best friends, Harvey and Valerie, called for me for school. I said bye to my aunts, Hilda and Zelda, and set off. At 9.20am (first lesson) I turned a dead frog into a live one. I also turned Libby into a goat because she was being annoying. In second lesson I didn't do anything except for work, work and more work. Third lesson I didn't turn Libby into anything, but I did turn the teacher into a frog. Last lesson I was messing about and I turned a girl called Sarah into a pineapple!

2nd April
Dear Diary,
I mainly did the same as yesterday, but today at 9.20am I was asking Valerie a question and she wouldn't speak to me. I asked her what the matter was and she said to me that she wasn't my friend. I was confused. I didn't know what I had done wrong. All through the day she was like this.
Goodnight Diary.

3rd April
Dear Diary,
At 9.20am, Harvey came up to me and told me that Valerie had fallen out with me because of yesterday when I turned Sarah into a pineapple. I think that I need to be more careful with what I do with my magic, it is only for important things.

Today for our tea we went out for a meal because it was my Aunt Zelda's birthday. She was six hundred and one today. I had a lovely time out.
Goodnight Diary.

Toni-Anne Ashcroft (12)
Pool Hayes Community School, West Midlands

FAME!

I stepped out of the car gracefully and was blinded by the dazzling lights of photographers. Reporters were screaming questions at me, children were crying and grabbing my arms, a girl was being held back by security, and all because of me.

The red carpet loomed before me like a dragon's tongue. One trip would be front page news. Being careful not to trip in my perfect, black, lace-up stilettos, I took a step forward. Out of the corner of my eye, I saw the fan break free of security. She sprinted towards me. I felt her arms fling themselves around my neck.

Then I was lying on the floor, dazed. A swirl of flashing lights and bulging men lifted me to my feet. I was whisked inside, given a glass of ice-cold Volvic water and asked whether I wanted to continue. I told them that of course I would, but I would have to get in touch with my agent.

No one refused, not that anyone ever does. So I was taken through back passages to the seating area, where the awards had already started.

It was time. They were calling out the nominees. I had already been told earlier that I was to win, but this didn't stop my stomach from squirming. My speech quivered in my trembling hands.
'And the winner is . . .'
Oh my God, is my hair OK? Should I change my speech? Too late. I tried to smile as I stared back at the crowd speechless and lost.

Rebecca Vaughan (12)
Ramsey Grammar School, Isle Of Man

A Day In The Life Of Me

I wake up to the piercing ring of my alarm clock. Hiding my head under the pillow, I've realised, doesn't make it stop.

When I finally manage to haul myself out of bed and into the shower, I begin to daydream. I dream about me and my band. I'm the drummer and I think of us on stage, rubbing shoulders with all those other talented people. Even thinking about it gets me excited! Maybe one day it will really happen. At the moment we just play gigs at local pubs and bars. I suppose you've got to start somewhere and there's been a good response so far but that could just be the locals not wanting to be mean.

We've even made a CD, but not one that's sold in the shops. That will be the day; one of our albums in the window at HMV!

Our band is different to most other 'rocky' bands because we are all girls. When we were at school and starting out, our spectators were mainly boys and I don't think the teachers actually expected us to stick at it, a craze; trying to be a 'hard girl'! But when we make it, look who'll be laughing then!

'Liana, will you hurry up and get out that shower! You've been dreaming again and are going to be late for school!'
Oh well, I suppose I better go and get ready. Maybe one day we will!

Sian Howes (12)
Ramsey Grammar School, Isle Of Man

A Day In The Life Of Dave Grohl

Yo! I'm Dave Grohl. Maybe you know me, maybe you don't. I'm ex-Nirvana drummer (so don't mess with me!) and creator and lead of Foo Fighters (we rock). I'm exhausted. Taylor - our drummer - insisted that we went on a pub crawl last night. Jeez Louise, we went to 12 pubs, 3 clubs and didn't get back to the hotel until 4am, after falling into several garbage cans on the way. We're on tour at the moment, so not such a good move!

My head is seriously killing me. It feels like I've been smashing it against a wall, and now Chris (guitarist) and Nate (bassist) are arguing about the set list. It's like:

Chris: 'Monkey Wrench!'
Nate: 'Headwires!'
Chris: 'Come on man. MW rocks!'
Taylor: 'We never play Floaty anymore . . .'
And me: '*Shut up!*'

I've started writing a new track, and I really want to play it with Jimmy Page (from Led Zep. He's my hero) but I've never met him so I've not really had a chance to ask about it!

We've got a gig later. We're touring with Red Hot Chili Peppers and I've been jamming with Flea and John. Flea really rocks. Once you've put a bass in his hands he's off, stringing out fantastic riffs. It's amazing.

I'm off shopping with Taylor now, he wants new shorts. All he ever wears is shorts and little else. I 'owe' him a pair apparently cos I put him in a bin last night. Hee, hee . . .

Katie Jones (13)
Ramsey Grammar School, Isle Of Man

FIRST IMPRESSIONS

What are all these shapes? Why is everybody clattering and wrapping me up? Why are there figures above, sniffing and splashing me with small water droplets? They are crying I think. I can feel something soft, warm and cuddly; people calling me Ashley and 'a little girl'. I don't know what a girl is. How can I be a girl?

Now, things aren't quite so confusing. I can recognise Mummy and Daddy by their smells. When I wake in the morning, all I see is my mobile. Then, out of the blue, I get this feeling. I start to cry. Why does Mummy know exactly what to do? She feeds me and then I stop.

I can see properly now. I love to find shiny objects and look into them. I see someone who looks just like me and copies me as well. Who is this person? I also remember motions now, like kissing and waving.

My body's a funny thing. I find new pieces of me every day. My favourite are my hands, they have wriggly fingers on them which I always seem to stick in my mouth.

I keep trying to hoist myself up, trying to stand. I can do a lot of things now without Mummy or Daddy's help.

People have come round to see me, giving me cards and boxes with shiny paper on. Now a cake with one candle on. What will happen next?

Shelley Harper (12)
Ramsey Grammar School, Isle Of Man

NEWSPAPER HEADLINE - 1665 - THE PLAGUE

The Plague Is Over!

The disease that has haunted London for the past year is being killed by the cold! The disease that made life in the capital a living hell, one in which millions died in filthy, stinking conditions, is itself being killed.

For months people have been living in a city which contained hundreds of thousands of people infected with a highly contagious disease which caused boils the size of tennis balls to cover the victim's armpits and groin. Sinister dark swellings covered the rest of the body. Coughing up blood and with breathing difficulties they would see the buboes on their own body burst and spew out thick black pus. Locked in their homes, the sick with the healthy, they all, millions of them, would die in agony.

Between them, in ten months, two strains of this disease have caused millions of deaths. The first, Bubonic Plague, causes the buboes and sinister dark swellings that cover the body. The second, Pneumonic Plague, causes the breathing problems and the coughing up blood and other gunk from the lungs. Catching either of these strains of the dreaded disease would cause certain death within a week. There is no effective cure for the disease or the terrible pain the victims suffer. Life in the city was awful.

With no entertainment there was nothing to give you the will to carry on living. The people fast gave up hope when someone in their family caught the plague. They would all be locked in together.

Graeme Osborn (13)
Ramsey Grammar School, Isle Of Man

THE MAKING OF MANN

Many years ago the world was ruled by giants. These giants fought ferociously. There was an Irish giant called Finn MacCooil who was fighting a great red-haired Scotch giant who came over to challenge him. Finn could see the Scot was escaping so he grasped a great handful of soil to slow the Scot down. He threw it and missed, but the great lump cascaded into the Irish sea. This formed an island - now called the Isle of Man and the crevasse from where the great mass came from is now Lough Neagh.

You may know the story is true because the Irish have always looked on the Isle of Man as a parcel of their own. They say that when Saint Patrick blessed the soil of Ireland and all the creatures that might live upon it, the power of that blessing was also cast upon Mann.

Saint Patrick was a mighty man,
He was a saint so clever,
He gave the snakes and toads a twish!
And banished them forever.

And there is proof of the truth and the saying to this day, for while such nasty things do live in England, they cannot breathe freely on the blessed soil.

Adam Millard (12)
Ramsey Grammar School, Isle Of Man

A Day In The Life Of A Victorian Child

I was woken by the other apprentices early in the morning. They had increased their voices from quiet, to normal, to loud. I think they were arguing about whose house to go to, to sweep their chimneys. I was part of a group of young children aged from five to fourteen, I think. All of us were orphans and had to work as apprentices for a living. As one of the youngest and smallest I always got the narrow chimneys to sweep. So it was on this particular day that changed everything.

I was with my boss, Mr Zabina, and we went first to Mrs Flanagan's house. That was a very thin chimney, and after that we went on to Mrs Richie's, Mr Dickinson's, Mr Jones' and finished at Mrs Jackson's, where Mr Zabina said I did a great job in the wet and windy conditions. Two of the chimneys hadn't been swept for about two years either.

As we were walking home, Mr Zabina was attacked by a group of men who took our brushes and beat him up quite badly. I didn't know what to do so ran back to the orphanage for help. Everyone shouted at me as if it was my fault, which made me cry. I was kicked out onto the street and that night I froze to death.

Terry Ayres (13)
Ramsey Grammar School, Isle Of Man

THE LADY OF AYRES

As the sun begins to set on the Ayres and the shadows begin to lengthen, a ghostly figure can be seen running on the distant horizon.

The ghostly figure has no name but she was once a woman of great beauty. However, now there is just a scared and bewildered face. You can see her at night as she runs across the horizon in a grand blue dress that looks late Victorian. She wears no shoes and her dress is torn many times, as is her face and feet.

She is always out on Friday 13th. Often people report that she comes up to them and says, 'Help me, you've got to help me. He's after me. Help me please!' She then runs off into the night, constantly looking around as if she were being followed.

There were countless searches and digs in the 1890s to find a body or a clue, but all of them were unsuccessful. The only hint they could find was a piece of blue silk material which was snagged on a bramble bush near the wood.

All the newspapers from the 1890s in Great Britain have been searched for a clue to whom this woman might be, but there were no advertisements or pictures to match her ghostly face.

Many have tried to guess the gruesome fate that befell the poor girl, but guessing is all they can do. To all intents and purposes, she never existed.

Samantha Westcott (13)
Ramsey Grammar School, Isle Of Man

MANX FAIRIES

Have you ever believed in fairies? It's not unusual or strange whatever age or gender you are. Children and adults alike believe that when a tooth falls out you should wrap it up and put it under your pillow. While you're sleeping a fairy will fly into your bedroom and take the tooth back to the fairies' bridge in Santon, leaving behind some money.

When the journey is over, the fairies pull together to polish all the teeth and deliver them to the post fairy, who takes them high in the sky and places them one by one in the sky. At that stage they are called stars and if you ever look up and see a 'shooting star' it's not a star, it's a post fairy.

Tip: If you are ever in the Isle Of Man and drive past the fairy bridge, *always* say hello. If you don't, it's been known your car wheel will puncture or the petrol will run out. Another thing visitors do is write messages to the fairies and put them on the trees round about.

Remember, it's not a 'shooting star', it's the post fairy.

Kimberley Counsell (12)
Ramsey Grammar School, Isle Of Man

THE DAILY SNAIL

Elves Are Alive

People walking through the woods of Snaefall last night saw one or possibly two elves!

We sent our reporter to investigate this sighting further.

The people who had seen them were two farmers from Wolverhampton, England and on holiday in the Isle Of Man. Apparently they were just walking through the forest and all of a sudden saw two mystical creatures that were very small (in books, however, the elves are very tall . . . aren't they?). Well, we decided to talk to the two farmers to investigate this further.

Daily Snail: 'Now gentleman, what were these spectacular creatures like? What I mean is were they enchanting, magical or, well, just give us a description of them.'

Farmers: 'I don't know, we didn't see anything, somebody must have just told you that we had seen them. By the way what are we talking about here mate?'

Daily Snail: 'The elves you saw.'

Farmers: 'We haven't seen any elves . . . well recently anyway. Though we did see a tiny little man in Maughold.'

Daily Snail: 'So you didn't see any elves.'

Farmers: 'No we didn't see any elves!'

It would appear that our reporter flew to the Isle Of Man for nothing but we will continue to investigate the matter further.

In other news Mrs Jones from Ramsey Grammar School has been found *not* guilty of reversing her car over two elves on the mountain road! Apparently she could not see them through the mirror.

Christopher Smith
Ramsey Grammar School, Isle Of Man

THE BUGGANE OF ST TRINIANE'S

A very well-known Manx Tale is the Buggane of St Triniane's which explains why the church has never had a roof.

The church was called Keeikll Brisht, the broken church, by the old Manx people because they said it was never finished. It wasn't that they didn't try to put a roof on, but every time they tried a terrible Buggane rose out of the ground and brought it crashing down.

It is said that a tailor called Timothy made a bet with the local people that when the roof was finished he would stay in the church and make some trousers.

At night when they left the villagers lit a fire of rowan branches which made a blue smoke that protected them from evil, but he forgot to keep it alight.

He sat there in the church sewing until he reached the last seam when, with a terrible roar, the Buggane slowly came up from the floor. The Buggane kept threatening Timothy but he took no notice and kept going. It had a head of coarse black hair and eyes like torches and he got very cross. Timothy finished his sewing and jumped out of the window and ran away down the hill as the roof came crashing down behind him. The Buggane chased him all the way to Marrown church where he was safe. The Buggane was so cross he tore his head off and threw it at Timothy where it exploded.

Timothy lived to tell the tale but the Buggane didn't and no one has tried to put a roof on since.

David Hicks (13)
Ramsey Grammar School, Isle Of Man

A DAY IN THE LIFE OF A SOLDIER

We were in the trenches shooting across no-man's-land towards the Jerries. There was forever the sound of gunshot, firing noises and shells landing near us. There was no peace, only noise. I had had enough so I decided to move closer to no-man's-land and as I did so, a shell landed in the trench I had just vacated.

I ran to the closest trench and jumped in. Two soldiers there already were dead, shot by German artillery. I got my rifle out and started shooting, just shooting until I ran out of ammunition. I then purloined the rifles of the other two soldiers.

I found myself wanting to get closer to the Jerries, so I ran to yet another trench where I found two of my mates, Bob and Billy. I was tired and in need of a drink, but we had to keep firing. One foolish German stood up and I shot him without even thinking.

Suddenly I heard a different sound - a plane! It was a good old English Spitfire; in fact there were three of them. They fired on the Germans and allowed us to advance successfully. We had got closer to Berlin and tonight we could sleep.

Daniel Oram (13)
Ramsey Grammar School, Isle Of Man

THE GOOD OLD DAYS

This is a short story about a pet dog dying.

Lassie, why did you leave me? Why did you die? I couldn't bear to look at you. So pathetic and useless. So much pain. I can't imagine the pain.

Even the day died when you did. You were so obedient. Came when you were called, sat when you were told to. You were so good to me.

You were old and exhausted but I loved you.

I remember the old days. Just me and you. Running in the park. I will never forget those days. The good old days.

You had four playful puppies. I remember it so clearly. We were all so proud of you. You were proud too. You looked after them so well, I cared and loved them the way you did.

Signs of old age suddenly jumped onto you. Over the years you started to slow down, not so energetic. You lost your hearing and voice gradually. It was then I loved you more. But you were still so wonderful and so caring.

I remember the nights you sat on my bed, listening to all my stories. I remember the long walks we went on together. I know you loved me. It was a special kind of love and I could not have been happier with another dog. It would have to be you.

But now you are gone. I know you will wait for me in Heaven. I am never going to forget you or the good old days. Yes, the good old days.

Vikki Knight (13)
St Anne's School, Alderney

HALLOWE'EN HORROR

It was the 30th of October, on a dark, stormy night. My mum was working a night shift at the hospital. I wasn't in the mood to answer the door for the trick or treaters. I decided I would just shout 'get lost' and they would go away, but there was somebody that night who didn't.

They persistently rang the doorbell and then everything went eerily silent. I pulled the curtain aside and peered out to see who it was; but there was no one there. I sat down and then the ringing started again. I charged to the door and flung it open and yet again there was no one there. As I turned around, I saw something out of the corner of my eye . . .

A shiver ran up my spine. I was too scared to turn around, but I knew I had to. I slowly turned to find my mother lying motionless on the doorstep; a nail right through the centre of her forehead. Attached to the nail was a note with the words 'I'm going to get you' scribbled on it in red ink.

I slammed the door shut and ran to the phone. My hands were trembling as I was trying to press the right keys for 999. My heart almost stopped as I heard the long lasting beep that signalled the phone was dead.

Stepping back from the phone I ran into the kitchen to lock the back door, when I realised that it was already wide open. That was when I knew there was somebody in the house other than me. I noticed a note on the fridge, I ran over to read it. It said 'I'm getting closer'. I turned around to run to the door but he had already locked it and was holding the key in his hand!

Lianne Bunn (12)
St Anne's School, Alderney

UNDER HER WINDOW

It was a dark night. The street lamps hadn't been working for some time now. Katy knew she shouldn't have watched that horror movie at Sam's house. She was playing the scenes over and over in her head, which didn't help on the long walk home.

She stopped to tie her shoelace right next to a big dark bush. She was just about to get up when she heard the leaves crunch in the undergrowth. She didn't need anything else to happen, she was scared and the fact that her boyfriend had just died was a great coincidence. However, what she didn't know was that it was in fact her boyfriend's ghost in the bush. He had been following her since the car crash; he wanted revenge for her leaving him and letting him die.

Katy ran all the way back to her house after the strange noises, slammed and locked the door, then ran up to her bedroom and hid under the covers.

That night she woke up frozen stiff in her bed; she could hear that same rustling in the bush beneath her window. The curtains were blowing in the wind, Katy could have sworn she had closed the window, but she was too scared to close it now.

Ellie Gaudion (13)
St Anne's School, Alderney

IN A JUNGLE SOMEWHERE

It was a great day to be flying over an island made up of unexplored forests, it was sunny and not even a slight breeze was blowing. Ralph Johnson was flying with his mum and dad in their plane.

Ralph noticed that the engine was making some noise, so he went to tell his dad. He didn't even make the cockpit when it exploded! He fell to the floor and his ears were ringing and the plane started to descend.

Ralph and his mum grabbed the parachute, while his dad said that he would try to land the plane.
'No, don't,' Mrs Johnson screamed. 'Come with us!'
'I have to,' he replied.
They landed in the forests near the coast. They decided to walk towards, and eventually around, the coast.

On their way to the coast they came across an old hut. It couldn't have been occupied since World War I and was in a terrible state. It was made of nothing but wood and nails. They stayed there for a bit and then went on to reach the coast.

They also found some debris from the plane. It looked like the propeller. Mrs Johnson began to cry.

They began to walk, they didn't know where, but they knew where they wanted to go.

Iain Macfarlane (12)
St Anne's School, Alderney

EVERYBODY HAS A DARK SIDE
(A short story about strange discoveries)

It was early evening when Timothy answered his mobile to find out the strange news. At first he couldn't quite believe it. A secret society formed by celebrities all over the world to worship the Devil.

He worked furiously because he knew that he only had eight hours before the national newspapers found out about this. Timothy needed names, meetings and locations, anything that would prove that this rumour was absolutely true. He needed to be the first to sell his story. It was his last chance to save his reputation as the best, most hard-writing journalist in the industry.

Several hours later, he stared at the web page in front of him. *Timothy Major*, he thought, *you are a genius.* He'd managed to hack into the society's home page. Names leapt off the page at him. Timothy clicked onto the history page.

It had all started ten years ago. The founder was Michael Jackson who encouraged other famous musicians, actors and actresses, TV presenters and some ordinary people to join his strange new cult.

It met every month in different countries. They performed rituals which included burning Bibles and crosses. Each new member took part in an induction ceremony in which they pledged to only worship the Devil.

He had acquired all the information that he so desperately needed. It was time to ring round all the editors of all the newspapers he could think of. He knew that he would have to work hard to convince everyone that this information was true, but he was ready to fight for his front-page story.

Lauren Jean (12)
St Anne's School, Alderney

THE BATTLE WAR

As the sun rose I awoke. It was a beautiful day, but this was going to be unlike any other day I had experienced before, because today was the day of the battle. I won't say where the battle is because it could be anywhere in the world. It could be in the past, the present or the future.

It was going to be a brutal battle of hand-to-hand combat. I knew in my heart that a lot of people would be killed on both sides.

I tried to eat some breakfast but felt sick with nerves just thinking about the battle ahead. I started to sweat. As I made my way to the battlefield, the hairs on the back of my neck stood on end. I could hear screaming and yelling. I started to run towards the fighting but my legs started to feel like lead. Before I knew it I was in the middle of the battle, fighting for my life.

Suddenly there was a strange silence. The battle was over and I was still alive. Victory was ours, but it didn't feel like it. If that was war I never wanted to go through it again. And I would never want anybody else to go through the horror of battle, or world war, ever again.

Jennifer Bohan (13)
St Anne's School, Alderney

WEIRD CREATURE ATTACKS MANHATTAN

Yesterday at 12.00, during the carnival, a weird old man came screaming down the road. He was screaming, 'It's a monster'. 1 minute later, a big T-rex came thudding down the road. It stopped, then it roared and bit a sixty-foot building. People were jumping out of the same building and screaming.

So far he has killed 50 people. I witnessed this attack, it was so terrifying that I have been going to a psychiatrist for the past few days. He says I'm mental, I have to take pills, but I haven't because I think I'm not mental. I don't care what they say. Right . . . back to the story.

The army are planning an attack tomorrow, 9pm at the subway. They think the creature has laid eggs there. The army's mission is to kill the eggs and the creature. They might bring in the Royal Marines and the CIA to help. Also there is a meeting tonight at the White House. The president will tell the press what the plan is, to kill the creature and the eggs.

The creature or, 'Rex' as they call him, has destroyed the Manhattan Park, 5 skyscrapers, 20 houses and a train station. In my opinion this creature is the worst thing that has happened to Manhattan ever.

Stephen Blondin (11)
St Anne's School, Alderney

A BAD DREAM

I woke up after having a really bad dream. I got up and looked for my mum. No one was there, only Jim and Ranger, the cats. I got dressed and went out to the garden. Everything was wet and I remembered that the night before there had been a storm.

I was looking down at the ground, not really focusing on anything, then I saw footprints in the mud. I followed them into the trees and around a stream. I'd never been this way before, but I followed the footprints anyway. After a while I came to a cave. I looked in and found out that it must go right to the back of the hill. I ducked down and entered. When my eyes adjusted, I started walking down the largest tunnel.

It felt like I'd been walking for hours and when I came to a turn in the tunnel, I wished I'd stayed at home. Up against a wall were the bodies of my neighbours and friends from the village. They were all dead. Suddenly something caught my eye. I thought it was a man at first, but I soon realised it wasn't. It approached me and when it came close enough, it threw a knife at my head. Just as the knife was about to stab me I woke up. I'd just had a really bad dream. I got up and looked for my mum. No one was there, only Jim and Ranger, the cats.

Bonnie Flewitt (12)
St Anne's School, Alderney

THE HAUNTED HOUSE

One night, a long, long time ago, a young girl named Michelle Johnson snuck out of the house. She was only ten years old, a bit young to be adventuring out alone, especially during the night, but anyway, she decided to go to the house at the top of Horrormount Hill. People say it's haunted, so Michelle decided she wanted to find out whether it was true, or whether people just said it to try and scare her.

She walked and walked for about twenty minutes and then, there it was right in front of her. She walked up to the front door. She was scared. She was terrified, terrified about what might happen to her if it was haunted. Terrified that she might get killed by a ghost, but still she walked towards the door. She knocked on the door to see if a cleaner or someone was there. No answer, so she put her hand on the handle and suddenly . . .

A man with a knife jumped through the doorway. Michelle jumped back and screamed instantly.
She said, 'Please don't kill me Sir, I'm only ten years old.'
'Oh, I'm sorry my dear, I thought you were someone else,' he replied.
'Who did you think I was?' she exclaimed.
'I thought you were the one we call 'The Ghost Of Horrormount Hill'. He comes every night, he haunts this place,' he replied.
'So it's true, it is haunted,' she declared.
'It sure is,' he said, taking a gulp at the same time.
'OK, OK, my friends have told me that it is haunted, but I didn't believe them, so I thought I would come up here and find out for myself, once and for all,' she said.
'So now that you know, you can go home and think about something else.'
'But I was rather hoping to get a look around, you know, find out what it's like inside. May I?' she asked.
'No, you definitely may not,' he replied.
'But why not?' Michelle asked politely.

He replied, getting rather angry at this stage, 'Because I said you can't. Now hurry along home, go on, get out of here.'
'OK, I'm going, I'm going,' she exclaimed, very scared, I might add.

She ran all the way home and snuggled up into bed and went to sleep. Now she knew the truth, it was haunted, and she would go and tell all her friends at school the next day.

Kirsty Walters (12)
St Anne's School, Alderney

The Vampire Killers

The door creaked open. We walked down the steps into the dungeon. It was dark and gloomy and the only light was coming from a small crack in the wall. I could hear mice in the corner.

'The vampire is down here somewhere,' said David quietly.
Then out of nowhere a vampire appeared and shouted, 'Are you looking for me?'
I was petrified. As the vampire looked for anyone else, I ran as fast as I could out of the dungeon, through the graveyard and into my car. I drove as fast as I could and it only took me five minutes to get home instead of fifteen minutes.

The next day, I went back to the castle with a gun loaded with silver bullets. I then went down to the dungeon and looked on the floor. David was lying on the floor, dead, with teeth marks in his neck.

I went to the police station and told them everything. The police went to the castle to see what had happened. They said that they would try to catch the vampire, but it was not going to be easy. I went back to my flat, then rang David's parents and told them the bad news.
All David's mum said was, 'I knew the job was going to kill him one day.'

The next day, I was driving along the road that was opposite the castle when I saw a gravestone with my name on it. I got out of the car and went to the gravestone to get a better look. I turned around to get back in my car when a vampire jumped out from behind a gravestone with a gun and shot me.

Liam Sumner (11)
St Anne's School, Alderney

THE MAD SCIENCE TEACHER

It was a typical day in the science lab. Mr Langley was telling off the Year 9s and Mr Williams was testing some science liquids. Mr Langley got annoyed with someone (not mentioning any names) and mixed cloroxide and floroxide together, purposely adding the secret ingredient.

Ten minutes later, he ran into assembly shouting, 'I wasn't thinking straight, I knew the consequences, but mixed them up anyway!'
'Mixed what up?' asked Mr Philips. 'You mixed what up?' sounding anxious.
'I saw the light, I saw it.'
'Sawvwat?' asked the French teacher, Madame Johnson.
'A-a-a huge rat!' he answered.
All the children screamed and the teachers looked at each other. The children went home for the rest of the day. What they didn't know was that the teachers suddenly mutated into super heroes and went to fight the rats.

There were two main rats that hid in the cellar of the school. However, after the teachers had morphed, the rats had had three thousand babies. The teachers couldn't handle the rats so they called in 'The Beastly Boys Super Hero Gang' which consisted of Rhys, Ashley, Liam and Iain.

They all took their BB guns. They knew that plastic wouldn't kill the rats, so they dipped the ball bearings in a sleeping powder and shot the bullets in the rats' mouths so they would fall asleep. Then they got a lorry, got all the rats and chucked them off a cliff.

The Beastly Boys were praised and the mad science teacher was sent to jail.

Rhys Jenkins (11)
St Anne's School, Alderney

QUICK ACTION

'Three weeks ago, Scraps the Golden Retriever and Ziggy the tabby cat went missing from 72 Macintosh Street. Their owner, Mrs Raincoat, is very worried. We asked her how she felt.'

The television flickered quietly, Mandy watched eagerly. She really enjoyed Animal Action (it was her favourite show).

Mrs Raincoat came on in a flood of tears. 'Most people who own a pet don't mind letting them out in the garden to play. I didn't until last night. It was an ordinary night when I let Ziggy and Scraps outside to play, but when I went to call them in they weren't there, I was so worried and I still am.'

'Thank you Mrs Raincoat. Join us again next week to see what happens!'

Suddenly Mandy got a phone call from her mum.
'Mandy! James just rang, meet him at Modder Rhu Road, it's urgent!' her mum said.
'OK but . . . when?' Mandy questioned.
'*Now!*'
'OK, I'm gone!' Mandy dropped the handset into the cradle and ran out the door. When she was halfway down the road she saw that she had forgotten to put on her shoes! She ran back home and got her shoes on.

When she got to Modder Rhu Street, James was in a bush!
'James! What are you doing?' Mandy asked.
'Shh! Come over here,' whispered James.
'Why?'
'Just come.'
Mandy went over to James. *What is he doing?* Mandy thought. When she looked into James' arms she saw Ziggy!

'Ziggy!' she yelled. '*Scraps!*' she yelled again when Scraps came out from a hole in a tree.

When Mrs Raincoat got Ziggy and Scraps back, she was over the moon. She rewarded both Mandy and James £500 each. They were all really happy and so were Ziggy and Scraps!

Nicola Crawford (11)
St Anne's School, Alderney

WAR ON IRAQ

A Black Hawk helicopter has been shot down over southern Iraq. The eleven people on board have died and the families have been informed of their deaths.

The navy boats have been very busy firing Scud missiles into Baghdad, also into Basra. The aircraft carriers have had an important role in the war on Iraq by supplying plans to go and help bomb Baghdad.

There have been a lot of anti-war protesters in the streets of London, and also in Sydney, Australia, but the last one in London had a lot of schoolchildren in the protest.

Ryan Murray (11)
St Anne's School, Alderney

CHAPTER THREE

The First Day Back At School After Half-term

I was in a deep sleep, when all of a sudden, I jumped out of bed. It was my alarm clock. My clock woke me up at 7.30am to get ready for school. I didn't like my school because today I had boring lessons.

I got off the bus. I was bursting to go to the toilet. I strolled over to the wooden double doors, when suddenly, they opened. It looked frightening inside. I walked down the corridor, the lights were flickering in my eyes. To my left were the ladies' toilets. I opened the door with my shaking hands.

I pulled the flush. It didn't work. I continuously pulled the flush down. My arm was aching. It was very strange. I unlocked the door and I walked over to the sink, staring at myself in the mirror.

I looked deeply into the mirror. I heard the toilet door click open. I was terrified. I quickly turned around and looked at the door. It opened. I felt relieved, it was only Sophie, who was in my class. I turned back round to look at my reflection. I felt dirty. I turned the cold and hot taps on.

When the sink was full with water, I put my hands into the clear, rippling water and splashed water on my face. It was strange, I didn't feel anything. I stared at myself in the mirror. My face was dry. There wasn't any water trickling down my pale face.

Suddenly, the girl came out from the toilet and stood behind me. There was only one sink in the bathroom. Sophie had disappeared. I told myself to calm down. When I looked to see if she was behind me, I saw this great big, loud flash. It was her . . .

Gemma Johns (13)
St Anne's School, Alderney

A Day In The Life Of Beyonce Knowles

I woke up this morning to find a delicious American breakfast waiting for me.

After breakfast I went to the Jacuzzi and relaxed for a bit, while the waiter kept refilling my champagne glass. Then Kelly and Michael came round. Kelly told me about her new single 'Stole' and she gave me a copy.

We all went out to town and got some new shoes and some new clothes. We all thought it would be a good idea to go on holiday because we had been so busy recently. We decided to go to Hawaii on our private jet. Our flight is in 3 months' time on the 15th of October at 1pm. After booking our flights we went to a really nice restaurant and I had millionaire salad, caviar and champagne. We spoke about how comfortable our jet looked. We all had our own bedrooms, a lounge, a kitchen and we had one waiter each.

After lunch we went to my house for a swim in the pool. Then we dressed up in our best clothes and went out to meet Kelly's boyfriend. I wore my light blue cords and a shiny silver top with a belly chain. We went to a restaurant called 'Famous', but once we sat down the press came and took pictures and asked questions. We asked the owner to get rid of the press.
He said, 'No, the more customers the more money, you leave if you're annoyed.'
Kelly got annoyed with him and swore she'd get him back.

We went through the kitchen to leave and saw maggots in the meat and cockroaches in the rice. We went and complained to the food inspector and they got shut down.

Adele Woodruff (12)
St Anne's School, Alderney

A Day In The Life Of Corporal Samantha Gaudion

Dear Diary,
Another night of bombing!
Today is quite a quiet day (not), but last night was a night of hell for all of us. I know we've had bad nights but this one was of the worst, if not *the* worst, but one thing's for sure, the war is going our way!

I got a letter from my daughter saying how much she missed me, she said that she'd got me a teddy with an army suit and she called it Corporal Gaudion after me. I was so touched and I nearly cried!

Anyway, last night was horrific, the bombing was *so* loud (remind me to buy some earplugs). At the moment I'm really worried about what's going to happen to me. What if I don't make it, am I going to die? All these thoughts are running through my head (it's making me mental!) Also, at the moment, my colleagues are destroying statues of Saddam Hussein!

I doubt that I will be able to write in my diary again because we will be fighting every single second of the day. I have to go now because Sergeant is calling, so *bye!*

PS: I want Saddam Hussein dead and I want to free his people and I want this war over and done with!

Samantha Gaudion (11)
St Anne's School, Alderney

Scary Trip

One day six cub scouts went out to the forest to camp. While they were there they had loads of activities to do. They split into groups and went off and did them. They planned to meet back at the camp at 5 o'clock.

When 5 o'clock came, only two groups came back to camp. They waited until half five but there was still no sign of the others. When 6 o'clock came, they heard a scream and footsteps in the leaves. It was one of the cub scouts.
He went screaming to the leaders, shouting, 'It ate the others.'
The leader said, 'What did?'
'The monster.'
'What monster?'
'The bush monster that just jumped out on us.'
'Right,' said the leader, 'I am calling the safe services to come and pick us up. Get your stuff and come and get on the bus.'

'OK, is everyone here . . . yes . . . good.'

On the way home, the leaders called all the mums and dads to say that their sons were dead. They were driving through the trees when they saw it again, it was the monster with the big drooling teeth. It was carrying something but they could not quite make it out. It was shaking, then they knew what it was, it was one of the other group.
They shouted, 'Stop! There is it, the monster.' They pointed it out to the leader. It took a little while to see again. When they saw it, everyone went, 'Wow!'

The leader ran out of the bus and into the forest. Everyone waited for about five minutes then two bodies got thrown out onto the bus window. Everyone screamed and the bus driver stepped on it.

Joseph Gaudion (11)
St Anne's School, Alderney

A DAY IN THE LIFE OF THE LOCH NESS MONSTER

Nessie was sleeping soundlessly on his bed on April 4th, however he soon was up and about. After a hasty breakfast he rose to the surface, splashed to the jetty and, to his horror, saw a sign.

Loch Ness monster
£1,000 reward
Must be alive!

He didn't understand why everyone wanted to catch him. Nessie destroyed the sign and went off for a swim. He swam and swam far away from the jetty, he swam where the water grew salty. The sun's golden rays seemed to glow right through him, dazzling his scales. He forgot about the sign, he forgot about everything!

Nessie avoided a dog that was splashing madly near the shore, and lay happily sunbathing on the water for a while. Soon he began to get hungry so he snatched kelp off a rock for starters, then dived underwater to catch some fish.

After lunch, Nessie swam further towards the ocean and heard human voices! Two people were talking on top of a big stone on the shore, a third smaller human was walking over the pebbles near the water. As Nessie watched, the little child fell in the water but the others didn't notice! Nessie hesitated, remembering the sign, but in the end he sped up to where the human was struggling in the water and nudged her. She flew out of the water and fell on the shore. The two on the rock ran down to meet her. Nessie, however, had already swam off home; no one was going to get that £1,000 today!

Hannah Llewellyn (12)
St Anne's School, Alderney

WAR ON SADDAM

The war on Saddam Hussein has been bloody and they say it is going to get even more bloody when they reach the capital, Baghdad. US soldiers say that they are ten kilometres (6 miles) away from Baghdad, which has been attacked heavily by air assaults over the last week, which will be followed by a heavy ground attack.

The morale of Saddam's troops is said to have been boosted by the downing of two US aircraft, a Black Hawk helicopter and a one-man F/A-18 Hornet - the first fixed-wing aircraft to be brought down by enemy fire.

The friendly fire (blue-on-blue) in Iraq has been unbelievable.

'Friendly fire' has claimed the lives of two airmen from RAF Marham and three soldiers. Two RAF pilots died when an American Patriot missile near the Kuwaiti border shot down their GR4 Tornado. Lance Corporal of Horse Matty Hull, on duty with Colchester-based 16 Air Assault Brigade, died when a US A-10 tank buster aircraft fired on two armoured vehicles. In a third incident, two British soldiers from Staffordshire - Corporal Stephen John Allbutt, 35, and 19-year-old Trooper David Jeffrey Clarke - were killed when British comrades in another tank mistakenly fired upon their Challenger II tank.

A 6-month-old Iraqi baby, Mareyam Alan, suffering from burns sustained in a domestic house fire, has been flown to the UK to receive hospital treatment. Her injuries, which are unrelated to the conflict, required urgent life-saving treatment which could not be provided locally.

As a flight was leaving to bring casualties back to the UK, a decision was made on humanitarian grounds to include Mareyam on the flight. Mareyam and her parents were flown to Cyprus by the RAF and then on to Liverpool. She is currently receiving specialist treatment.

Matthew Collins (12)
St Anne's School, Alderney

CHAD'S REVOLT - THE FOLLOW-UP TO 'KILL SADDAM'

Saddam was once known as a friend to us, now we think of him as an enemy. As time goes on there will be the most horrendous war the world has ever seen between Iraq and the allies, Britain and America.

All of this is caused over suspected nuclear warheads hidden in Iraq. Britain and America tried earlier on to make peace, so this war would not go on, by sending in the UN weapons inspectors, but they were refused by the Iraqi leadership. When British and American weapons inspectors finally got into Iraq they found empty warheads which could do vile harm to those of Britain, America and Iraq. Britain are looking to send 3,000 troops and America are looking to send 3,000 troops. There will be F16s, Tankbusters, B52s, tanks, armed vehicles and there will be maybe 1,500 Turkish troops. When the vehicles arrive in Iraq it will be a long, tiring drive to the centre of Baghdad.

As more and more troops get sent into Iraq it could mean that more parents are losing their sons or daughters, and children losing their mums and dads. But all eyes will be focused on not killing innocent Iraqis. Although the journalists are not going to be in the thick of the action they must be cautious in case Iraqis come through towns and ambush them and capture them, or they could just come through towns and shoot them. But don't think this will be a total white wash, the Iraqis are bound to put up an excellent fight. The main part of this war is for the British and Americans to take over towns and oil links.

David Chadney (13)
St Anne's School, Alderney

THE DAILY TELEGRAPH

Abducted By Aliens

Today a school teacher from St Anne's school was abducted by aliens in a flying saucer and taken into the sky. The police are looking into the disappearance of the teacher but there is no evidence, all they have is an eye witness.

The teacher has long blonde hair with blue coloured highlights, she has brown eyes and was wearing a pink top, purple trousers and white trainers when she went missing. She was last seen on CCTV camera footage at LE Coqs stores heading towards Little Street. If you know anything, please contact Crimestoppers on 01800 333 000

Reported by John Barman

Smoking Facts

Did you know that after every cigarette you lose 5 minutes of your life? After you stop you have got so used to having something in your mouth that you eat more and put on weight. People start smoking because they want to look like their mates. People die every 15 seconds in the world through smoking related illness.

Reported by George Green.

David Jennings (12)
St Anne's School, Alderney

BAGHDAD CRISIS

We have a crisis on our hands. Baghdad is totally surrounded by Iraqi troopers. There are approximately 3,000 to the north and 2,000 to the south. We have sighted these people and are trying to move in. I think we are waiting for the cover of darkness to send in 15 British SAS to track down the snipers. Then we are going for a full-scale attack. At the moment the Desert Rats are on the front line ready to attack just in case they spot us. About 50 of our soldiers have been executed and some have died in the battle for Baghdad. We are still trying to take over Iraq but we are outnumbered. Some of the civilians are equipped with weapons and are fighting against Iraqi troopers. We have nearly taken over Basra, there has been another casualty of friendly fire. 'This time we shot down a Harrier and the Iraqis beat the survivors to death'. We have had the biggest tank battle since World War II and we won. We have found that the Iraqi troopers have been executing our soldiers while we have been feeding prisoners and treating their wounds. We are trying our best to take over Baghdad and so far we are succeeding.

Matthew Smith
St Anne's School, Alderney

SHE IS EVERYWHERE

Let's go into the backyard and tidy up, but be very careful, don't ever make the magpie move. She's a creature of elegance and beauty, sitting there with grace and glory. You know she is always watching us, she is everywhere. She is Grandmother Magpie. I will tell you what my father and my older brother saw one day.

My father and my brother were working in the cornfield when this smart-looking gentleman was on a walk to our little village. Now, to get to our village there are two routes, a longer one and a shorter one. Now this man was in a rush so he was about to take the shorter route until my father interrupted.
'I wouldn't go down there. Everyone who goes down there will never return, for the sacred one is there.'
'Don't be so silly,' the man said.
'No, he's right, listen to him,' my brother said
The man did not listen, instead, the stubborn, smart man walked on.

Grandmother Magpie sang him to come, luring him on to where all the creatures will finish in the core of the Earth. Just like that man. The magpie is always there. She is everywhere.

Ryan Blaney (13)
St Edmund's Catholic School, West Midlands

HE'S EVERYWHERE

Oh no, that horrible crow's in our garden again. Go and shoo it away. No, do not shoo it away for that is the dark evil crow. Look at it, watching its prey very slowly. Do you know it's watching us too? I will tell you a story of that crow.

It all happened when my father and his friends were out hunting. It was a rabbit they were after. That's when his friend saw it, the great grandfather crow. It was just sitting there in the swamp. He started walking towards the swamp. None of the others could see the crow but they called out to him.
'Don't go that way, that is where the grandfather crow lives.'
He carried on. He could not help it, he was being lured into his nest, the horrible, dark nest, and the dark crow was laughing. The man was dragged away by the crow and never seen again.

I will tell you this, that you may understand why we love, fear and respect old grandfather crow for he is good, but he is also death. That's why you should not shoo him away. I will also tell you this, he is everywhere.

Angelo Franco (12)
St Edmund's Catholic School, West Midlands

SHE IS EVERYWHERE

Come now, let's just quickly tidy the house. No, what are you doing? You can harm any other mouse, but not that mouse. That is the mother mouse. Nobody dares to harm or even move the mother mouse. She stays in the corner of the room, looking around with her small blue eyes, judging each and every one of us. If you harm the mother mouse, strange and terrible things will happen. Let me tell you a little story about her.

The mother mouse is not as innocent as she looks. My sister was walking along quite happily when she accidentally got in the way of an old lady. This lady was bitter and old. Although she was beautiful on the outside, she was definitely ugly on the inside. She was not just an old woman, she was magical and she could perform spells, good and bad. She didn't like my sister for getting in her way. She was very angry and was about to put a spell on her. Through some miracle, a mysterious lady stopped her and made the witch a mouse instead. She followed my sister into my house. The spell lasts for 100 years, after which she will have her revenge.

She just sits there in the corner of the room. She is still waiting. *She is everywhere.*

Jennifer Galloway (12)
St Edmund's Catholic School, West Midlands

THEY ARE EVERYWHERE

Come on then, let's get cracking with this tree, I'm starving.

No, no, don't cut there. Can't you see the beehive? Look how busy they are, buzzing around. Yes, look, that one's the queen bee. Be careful not to disturb her.

You know, they keep an eye on us. In the day they are harmless, but in the dark, in the dark they appear and release their mythical powers. Listen, I will tell you what happened to a great friend of mine who did not know.

My father and I saw him pass. We called out and walked with him. We escorted him to our village. It was a long trek. At dawn, we set up camp. He offered to chop some wood for the fire. We had warned him about the queen and not to be tempted. We had been walking a long time.

Everyone knows what had happened. He came to the older trees. The queen winked at him. He stopped to talk. The powers urge you to come closer, closer and closer to the hive.
One voice said, 'Go with her, follow her!'
'No! Stop! Go back!' warned the other.
The stranger refused the second and followed. There was no going back.

The bees had outnumbered him and devoured him alive. Out of the light and into the darkness. A slow and painful death.

I tell you this, she is everywhere. They are everywhere. She is goodness, she is death. Waiting and watching, watching and waiting.

Cameron Chumber (12)
St Edmund's Catholic School, West Midlands

HE IS EVERYWHERE

Follow me to a quiet place, I will tell you a story.

Here is a picture of a snake, no, not just any snake, it may look like a normal python, but it isn't. I suppose that you could say that it's special, yes!

If you come across a snake like this, you should keep your distance. In its time it was a man, quiet and polite. Look out for him, you can tell if it's him by his slight lisp. He is usually alone. Don't disturb him, he will trap you, hurt you, kill you!

Be careful not to hurt him or he will hurt you in return. He is quick and will get you, no problem, like he did with the others! Injure them? He did more than cuts and bruises! 9 out of 10 didn't make it! That one only made it because of luck. How? He would wrap tightly around his victim and squeeze them as tight as he could, crushing them so they couldn't breathe.

I tell you this because you should know and understand why we respect but are scared of the python. Its poisonous curse could find you or me, you should always remember the snakes are nearly everywhere we tread. The python is always waiting for its next victim, day and night!

Ruth Ewins (12)
St Edmund's Catholic School, West Midlands

THE NIGHT OF THE MUTANT PALM TREES

The year is 2099. Then again, it always is. Why not 2100? It's a perfectly good year! It was at night. But then again, bad things tend to happen at night . . .

This happened in Neo-Walsall (why Neo? Why not 'Indigo-Walsall' or something?), where popping out for chips could cost you your life! Palm trees were now native in the region. A secret government plan was put into place the year prior, labelled 'Operation Let's-contaminate-all-of-these-trees-so-that-we-can-see-what-happens-and-deny-it-at-the-elections'. They smothered each tree with radiation (again, why radiation?) to see what happened. Most trees began to die, but . . .

'That night' was particularly dreary. A new car, the XX-Jaguar-Turbo-SX (always lots of Xs!) was being tested by itself. Typical. Anyway, the car was in good shape until a tyre split and crashed into . . . a palm tree. The car picked itself up and dusted off. A glimmer of red, presumably evil, flashed in the headlights. The car-robot tried to run, but was suddenly uprooted by a pair of sticky hands . . . the tree!

The car-robot tried to free itself, but failed miserably, as car-robots are known to do. The palm tree tossed the car over his 'shoulders' at an approximate 39 degree angle. Very accurate. This tree seemed miffed, and considerably so.

'Ouch! Well . . . I'll send my army of mutant palm trees over to your town. For revenge purposes. Hope you don't mind.'
'But . . .'
'Ah-ah-ah! No back talk! Now, what date are you planning to die?'
'Err . . . when Hell freezes over!'
'Right . . . let me put this in my planner . . .'

Anthony Cooke (15)
St Francis Of Assisi RC School, West Midlands

A Time To Sleep

A flash, a rumble, the strains of a song . . . it is time, it has finally come. My whole body is paralysed with fear; terror twists my being in such a way I can hardly breathe, hardly think. Tears well up in my eyes, blurring the world, somehow making it seem less real, less terrifying.

The patter of feet echo along the corridor and soon I see the silhouette of him standing at the edge of the bed. I have dreamed of this moment for so long, yet now it's here I cannot help but feel petrified. He pulls off his cloak, illuminating the room with his golden glow. I shield my eyes from the brilliance of his white gown, and when I look again, fluttering wings have appeared at his back, fanning me with their breeze.

He stretches out a pale, glowing hand, and my own trembling version nervously reaches towards him. As soon as we touch a wave of peace and happiness sweeps over me, and I hear a voice that I am sure no one else can hear.
It whispers, 'It it time.'

I float above my body momentarily, long enough to hear the frantic beeping of the machine dying to one monotonous drone; the rush of nurses and the final shake of a head from a young doctor. I think of my life, all ninety years of it . . . it's time to sleep, it's time to go.

Helen Keenan (13)
St Francis Of Assisi RC School, West Midlands

A DAY IN THE LIFE OF WW1 BARBED WIRE

I awoke this morning to the usual earth-shaking roar that forces awake the many troops along the lines. I could feel the sun on my metallic skin; the only refuge left to the battle-weary, half-dead zombies of the western front.

As the artillery forced my eyes open, a horrible sight fell before me.

I surveyed the scene, as I tend to do on these occasions. In the beginning I used to count the lifeless shells hung on myself and the land. In the end I simply lost count.

I felt something shivering. It was a man. His tag read 'Fletcher Blake' our minds seemed to connect as he felt his last moments . . .

I could picture a sunny Manchester morning. I could see a woman . . . Mrs Blake perhaps. She had just hung out her washing, blissfully naive of the dreaded telegram awaiting her.

I saw another picture. It was a tall room . . . a sign hung above it. 'Manchester Recruitment Office'. It was where this boy's nightmare began.

The scene ended. Young Fletcher had gulped his last breath. For half a mile of mud. That mud will be Fletcher Blake's resting place. May he guard his English land . . . forever.

David Shaw (14)
St Francis Of Assisi RC School, West Midlands

Waiting

The sandy dunes were slowly disappearing into the eerie darkness, with the wind screeching in the icy winter air. The sun was setting in the ashen sky. Soon it would be a grim darkness which would conceal the last traces of light. The wind's chilled air was brushing against the long grass ferociously and the seagulls were flying to their nests to get out of the cold.

Craig was huddled in the long grass to get out of the shivering wind. He was becoming apprehensive. To stop him thinking the worst had happened, he threw stones and tried to hit a tree but soon this became tedious. His baggy tracksuit bottoms started blowing in the wind. His hands were beginning to feel like glaciers so he thrust his hands into the pockets of his coat. There was a shuffling near him. He was petrified and hid in the long grass but it was only a rabbit. He chased it with wrath and after that he felt quite warm. Then he started to babble onto himself about where he could be.

Craig was becoming very distressed. 'Where are they?' he shouted. *They should have been here by now,* Craig thought. *I bet Jeremy's doing this on purpose, the spiteful little mummy's boy. Just because I beat him in our English test.*

He did say he was coming with his catapult to shoot birds. 'Where the Hell is he?' Then there was a sudden cry from near the wood, it sounded like Jeremy. Craig ran as fast as he could, flying through the long, dense grass. He shouted, 'Jeremy, is that you? Where are you?' Jeremy replied, 'I'm on the edge of the wood, quickly come, please!'

When Craig got there, Jeremy was sitting there with what looked like a broken ankle. Craig was frantically thinking what he should do, he'd never taken a first aid course in his life. He was wracking his brain. *What should I do?* he thought. It was going to get dark soon so he couldn't run for help, it would have been even harder to find him in the dark again.

On the ground there was a lot of rubbish, but there was a piece of rope and a polythene bag. Craig picked up the bag, filled it to the brim with leaves and fastened the bag onto Jeremy's ankle with rope.

While they were walking back, Craig asked, 'What happened?'

Jeremy said, 'I was running because I knew I was late. When I was running down the track, I hit a rock. I fell straight onto my ankle. It twisted around, the pain was excruciating. Then I shouted for you and you came running. Thanks a lot, I'm sorry I was such an idiot, I was jealous because you beat me in our English test.'

Craig replied, 'I thought you had tricked me into thinking that you were going to come.'

When the two boys finally got home, the moon was hidden behind the clouds and it was very wintry and windy. Jeremy was always grateful to Craig for waiting there, because it would have turned a lot worse for Jeremy if Craig wasn't there.

Chris Masters (14)
Sanday Junior High School, Orkney

WAITING

The branches were wrapped in small icicles which were glistening in the falling sun. The frozen earth was covered in a crisp blanket of December snow. The trees were continuously shivering in the ice-bitten air. A small creek, which was once mobile and trickling, was now iced over as a slippery solid. Now falling into darkness, all of this was being engulfed in a late evening fog.

Slumped against a tree in the falling snowflakes, someone stood stamping their feet to keep warm, stirring up the settling snow. The black, wet stubble on his face was starting to form small icicles. His hands were buried deep inside his deerskin coat. His face was being swallowed up by the smoke from a cigarette, it was the only substance he was getting heat from. His ears were buried under a fur-skin hat. Every breath that was made felt like knives stabbing at fragile lungs. The mysterious person was slowly being blotted out by the new flakes of snow.

Still waiting, the lonely person had one companion. His companion was his gun.

Just as the body was going to abandon his spot, he heard something rustling. Young pullets and clucking hens started to scream with all their might. A hunter was amongst them. A safety catch clicked. In a couple of bounds the farmer had reached the fence. Something flashed out of a shelter and shot behind a bush. The animal's mouth had been full of bloodstained feathers. For a minute or two, which seemed like hours, nothing happened. Chickens started scratching in the straw. The deadly gun was raised, loaded and aimed at one spot in particular.

A hunter was now being hunted. The fox had caused a lot of torment, but now all of it was going to stop.

Andrew Walls (14)
Sanday Junior High School, Orkney

WAITING

The rain was pattering on the roof, the wind was howling like a wolf. The litter was blowing around in circles, the lamps were flickering like a blinking eye on the cold ground. There was the faint shadow of a dog in the lamps. The snowman looked like it was winking at the cars as they were going so fast it was like whizzing lights.

There was a man standing by the fence. He looked so cold. He had an old hat on his head. He had a little stubby chin. I could not see his face because of the shadow of the hat. He put a cigarette in his mouth but whenever he tried to keep warm, the wind crept blowing in his face. Then he started to jog up and down on the spot. He looked so cold. I wanted to invite him in for a coffee, but I was not allowed to. Then he slipped his hand into his pocket and started to pull something out. What was it ?

It was a little piece of paper. There was a number on it - 082506 2509678.
A man came to Simon and said, 'What are you doing?'
Simon said, 'Waiting for a car, why?'

The man walked off again. The rain started to fall and he began to light a fire on the field. The fire went out because it was too wet. Then he got a bottle of beer and when he finished the beer, he shouted, 'How are you?' But no one was there. He was shouting to himself.

Luke Smith (14)
Sanday Junior High School, Orkney

JENNIFER LEE

19.04.06
Hi ya. I have got a story to tell you. Johnny might tell Josh about me, he overheard me talking to Katie about him, now he says he's going to tell Josh today in school. I'll update you when I come back

Thank goodness, Johnny didn't say anything to Josh, but it's really hard keeping my secrets away from him. He keeps asking what's wrong with me, saying, 'I know there's something, you're acting all weird'. I was about to crack and tell him everything, but I never did and that's the main thing.

20.04.06
I was about to tell Josh but then he dropped a huge bombshell on me. He's moving to London. I can't believe it. I need to think about this. I suppose I could tell him now that he's moving. I'll tell him tomorrow in school because I'm only in one of his classes so I won't have to see him as much. I really hope we don't fall out over this. I've got to go over to Katie's now, I'll tell you all about what happens tomorrow. Night, night.

21.04.06
I've told him and I didn't get the reaction I thought I was going to get. He told me he felt the same way and he was going to tell me the same thing. I'm so glad it all worked out.

Dawn Mackenzie
Sgoil Nan Loch, Isle Of Lewis

ALL ABOUT WOLVES

I like wolves because of the cubs and the way they play-fight with each other. The reason I decided to pick wolves for this story is because I know quite a bit about them.

My favourite wolf is the red wolf because I learned about them in my English project. Did you know that the red wolf is smaller than the grey wolf, but larger than the coyote?

Do you know how the red wolf got its name? Because of the red on its head, feet and its ears. The red wolf can weigh from 45 pounds to 80 pounds. In the pack, the leaders are referred to as the alpha pair - or the more dominant males in the pack. The red wolf's diet is white-tailed deer and racoons. When the red wolf is very hungry it will go for a herd of cattle. It will pick out the calves because they are vulnerable.

Wolves howl at the moon and to communicate with each other. Sometimes for food and sometimes as a threat to another wolf. There are about 100 different kinds of wolves in the wild and in national parks like Yellowstone. The red wolf was nearly wiped out by a disease called the Hooked Worm, but their numbers are now recovering.

Sean Mills (12)
Sgoil Nan Loch, Isle Of Lewis

A Day In The Life Of A Queen

Tweet, tweet! Arghhh! I had just woken up to hear the birds singing in the trees and I saw a face outside my 14th bedroom. It was the most comfortable room to sleep in, but sometimes the window cleaners were there when I woke up.
'Good morning your Majesty,' said Joanne, my lady in waiting.
'And a very good morning it is,' I said.
'So, what is on the schedule today?' asked Joanne.
'I'm going to Harrods, then tea with Tony (Tony Blair the prime minister), then a trip to Windsor to get the gloves I left there last week. Mind you, I could just go and buy another pair from Gucci.'

It was 11 o'clock. I was just having a walk in the gardens when a plane came swooping over the palace. A mad fan was screaming my name. Now I know I'm popular but, really, this was too much.

2 o'clock. I had just finished my lunch, smoked salmon with caviar and cream cheese on scones. It really was lovely but a bit bland for my exquisite tastes.

4 o'clock. I was sitting there listening to Tony babbling on about the rights of the country. I just wished that something exciting would happen once in a while.
'Isn't that right your Majesty?' asked Tony.
'Sorry, what was that?' I said.
'I was just saying, wouldn't it be fun to go bungee jumping?'
'What a preposterous idea! The Queen can't be seen jumping off bridges!' But secretly I just couldn't wait to try it out!

Elizabeth Macleod (13)
Sgoil Nan Loch, Isle Of Lewis

EGYPT DREAMING

Well, if I ever get to the end of this and I'm still alive, I'll be lucky. I've got through half the wall in the pyramid of Tutankhamun, the boy king of Egypt.

The wall told the story.

Oh boy king of Egypt, let your soul be with Ra, king of the gods of Egypt. Let Osiris guide you to the afterlife with good heart for here is the story of the path to the afterlife that awaits the boy king.

After the early death of the king, he was mummified and laid to rest in his tomb. His spirit went on the path where he met many dangers. His journey went on for many days and nights, never stopping for the hope to reach his goal. Ra saw his bravery and knew that he would get to the afterlife without fail.

At the ferry, Osiris was waiting for him. The boy king, happy to have got this close to the afterlife, prayed to the gods that might be protecting him.

After a day on the ferry, he reached the afterlife where all the kings and gods greeted Tutankhamun and praised him for his bravery and the reaching the afterlife. He remained forever more in great happiness.

Penny Curry (12)
Sgoil Nan Loch, Isle Of Lewis

MY ROAD TO SUCCESS

I am an ordinary schoolboy with a very good voice. I am in a folk group for the mod. A man from a record company heard about our folk group and we agreed to record our Gaelic songs onto a record. Soon, we were in for a surprise! Two days later we were told that over 34 million copies were sold!

Soon we had over £745,000,000! The bank manager's jaw nearly fell right down to the floor when we told him the amount of money we had!

A few months later our wishes came true. Elizabeth, Anne and Fiona went shopping in Paris, New York and London. Alexander and I bought the things we wanted the most, so Alexander bought a Ferrari!

But soon we were down to £2,500. We argued about money problems. We lost £2,400 when the bank was robbed which left us with £100. The only thing we could do was split up, but the rest refused to split.

We soon had financial problems with the credit cards. To pay off the debt would cost us over £60,000! We had to sell everything we had bought to pay off the debts. Unfortunately the shops Elizabeth, Fiona and Anne had bought their clothes from refused to give us a refund. After we paid off the debts, we were penniless. There was nothing we could do but just resign. Oh well, it was a boring job anyway!

John Macdonald (12)
Sgoil Nan Loch, Isle Of Lewis

OUR TRIP TO EARTH!

It started when we were playing footie on Pluto, where we live. Ziggy went and kicked our last football right off the planet! Seeing as this was our last football there was nothing else to do but to go and get it.

Our mum was away with the spaceship so we decided just to jump off! I know it's not the safest thing to do, but we went anyway. We stood on the edge and counted to three. 1, 2, 3 . . . *go!* Off we went, floating along.

Really far away we saw this round thing. Of course I didn't have my glasses on and Ziggy wouldn't notice, he's a bit dozy! We decided to go in that direction. As we got closer we realised that this round thing couldn't be our ball because it was getting extremely big. Just as we were getting really close I realised where we were. We were heading for Earth (or so I thought)!

You see, I really am blind and when we got closer, I realised it really was our football! We grabbed it and floated back home, back to our game of footie.

When we reached home, we got back to our game. It was a penalty to Ziggy 'cause he had complained and said that I'd fouled him. He took the shot and I was so close to getting it, but it went right over the goal, and you guessed it, right off the planet!

Fiona Mackenzie (12)
Sgoil Nan Loch, Isle Of Lewis

The Greatest

The post came through the letterbox. Just one letter.
'There's a letter for you Mum. It looks quite interesting.'
Mum's eyes lit up as soon as she opened that letter. She couldn't even speak. She passed me the letter and started to cry, not with sadness, but with joy! I read the letter.
I am happy to inform you you have won a trip to Brazil!
We were off on an all expenses paid holiday to Brazil in one week! There are not many times in your life when you can say that. My mum had entered a competition but never told me because she never thought we would win.

Two weeks flew by. I hardly got any schoolwork done because I was so excited!

We reached the airport and boarded our flight - first class! We were off to sunny Brazil.

On the third day of this fantastic experience it became more than just an experience, for I was about to meet the world's greatest footballer . . . Pele! I was practising my skills on the beach and he came up to me.
He said, 'You are a good footballer.'
Imagine the world's greatest footballer saying that! He asked me for a kickabout and I just looked at him, thinking, *is the sky blue?* We had a great time. He was really funny and I learned loads of new tricks and skills and took loads of pictures to show my mates. It was the greatest day of my life!

Alexander Mackenzie (12)
Sgoil Nan Loch, Isle Of Lewis

DON'T GO INTO THE WOODS ALONE

One day, Jennie, Chloe and Kathleen went for a walk. They went to the shop with a £10 note. They bought a bag of crisps each. They also bought two bottles of juice each. They started going along the road, it was a long, twisty, thin road.
Jennie said to Chloe, 'Let's take a little short cut. I'm sure Kathleen won't mind.'

Jennie started shivering, she said to Chloe, 'Are we lost?'
Chloe tried to keep a brave face but she knew that they were lost. She sat down on a rock. Jennie didn't notice and kept walking. Chloe looked up, Jennie was nowhere in sight. Chloe started running to see if she could find her.

Meanwhile, Kathleen was making her way to find some help. She heard a cracking noise in between the bushes. Suddenly, out of nowhere, a rat jumped out in front of her. She ran into the trees. She kept running for ages. Then she started walking backwards slowly and carefully. Then she got the fright of her life. She and Chloe had bumped into each other.

Jennie walked even deeper into the woods. She was shaking and then she decided to rest. She went into her bag to get her drink. Her bag was empty.

Kathleen and Chloe found a bottle of juice, it was Jennie's favourite. They started running, they found her make-up, her other juice, her crisps and her lucky teddy.

They decided never to split up on roads they didn't know again.

Jacqueline Laing (13)
Sgoil Nan Loch, Isle Of Lewis

SUPER AMANDA!

Amanda looked like an ordinary girl, but she wasn't. She had a secret. Nobody knew that she was really a superhero. Usually she lived an ordinary life - well as ordinary as you can be when you're a superhero. Nobody apart from her father knew the *real* Amanda. Often she got whisked off to save someone or some place.

S H Plodd was at Amanda's house the next day when she got home from school. He was her boss.
'The world needs Amanda!' he told her dad.
She rushed upstairs, got changed and took her *marmalade*. They flew away to a place that Amanda didn't know at all. As they flew he explained what had happened. Some aliens from planet 'Dodo' who had sneaked onto Earth had set up a machine to blow up Earth.

Amanda put on her superhero clothes and flew into the station where the machine was. She guzzled down half a jar and was ready for action! She jumped onto the top of the machine and somersaulted down. The aliens were scared. She punched a couple of them unconscious but a few wouldn't give in.

Suddenly she had an idea. *Marmalade!* She grabbed her jar and threw it with all her might. It exploded right on top of the machine and the main alien. He melted away on the spot. The machine started beeping.
'Failure, failure!'

She'd done it again. She'd saved the world!

Anne Macleod (13)
Sgoil Nan Loch, Isle Of Lewis

THE UNICORN AND THE LOCH NESS MONSTER

Sally, the unicorn, was bored and went to Loch Ness. Sally sat down on the ground and looked out at the sea, then she saw a big purple boat coming out of the sea. She saw it wasn't a boat but it was a Loch Ness monster. The Loch Ness monster was purple with blue spots. Sally was scared and ran from the loch.

Sally turned around and saw that the Loch Ness monster looked friendly. Sally walked towards the Loch Ness monster.
The monster asked, 'What is your name?'
The unicorn replied, 'My name is Sally, what is yours?'
He said, 'I'm Angus, the Loch Ness monster.'

Sally and Angus became friends. Angus told Sally that he and his family lived at the bottom of the loch near the old boat with the Scottish flag.

One day they were sitting near the loch and Angus said, 'Before I met you I thought that unicorns were very weird.'
Sally wasn't very happy with Angus, she told him, 'That wasn't very nice; I never want to see you again.' Sally went to the Unicorn's paper and told them everything that Angus had told her.

The next day, Angus was reading a paper that someone had left on the wall. He picked it up and saw a picture of himself. He was very shocked. He realised that people wanted to catch him. Angus went back to the loch and no one ever saw him come out of the loch ever again.

Karen Mackay (12)
Sgoil Nan Loch, Isle Of Lewis

THE SCHOOL

I had just arrived at a new school. I was so nervous that I could hardly speak. I was sitting in the car for about five minutes until I finally got the courage to step out. As soon as I stepped out I saw how big the school was. I turned to go back into the car but my mum had already driven off. I had no choice, I had to go in.

I opened the door and everyone stopped talking and looked at me. I didn't know what to do so I just kept walking. I had just taken a few steps when suddenly a teacher appeared. I froze on the spot.

The teacher had scruffy black hair, a torn jumper and a stained miniskirt. I was so scared that I could hardly breathe. Just as I was about to turn and run out the door the teacher shouted 'welcome' in a bitter, careless way and then she walked away. I stood there for a very long five minutes, then the bell rang. I didn't know where to go so I just followed some of the people that looked my age.

When I got to registration it was even worse. The teacher was wearing rags and she was smoking! I ran out of the school and screamed my head off and I never went back again.

David Robertson (13)
Sgoil Nan Loch, Isle Of Lewis

MY DIARY

14th July
Never guess what! Mum and Dad have decided to move - again! Not a little move but a big move - to China! I have only just got settled here in Scotland and have only just found new friends. I wish my dad wasn't a technician. If he wasn't he wouldn't be getting all these jobs all over the world. My parents don't seem to mind the fact that I might have a view on moving again. They just seem to think I have to go with it. At least I've got my diary to express my feelings. Well, it's 11.30pm and I had better stop writing because I've got to be up at 7.30am to start packing, my mother told me.

15th July
Have packed my things today and am ready to take the big step to move to China. I went round to see my friends today, they said that they would e-mail me all the time, but I'm still not happy about leaving. We go tomorrow on an early flight. Won't be writing much in here, I will be on the plane. My poor rabbit, it will be alone while we are travelling. What can I do? I just have to go along with whatever my parents say, I don't seem to have a choice.

3rd August
Arrrgh! I hate my life. School is horrible, people are teasing me. Life is going to be so hard for me, especially if Dad is changing jobs all the time.

Ruth Sara Mason (13)
Sgoil Nan Loch, Isle Of Lewis

THE MYSTERY MONSTER

Once upon a time there was a boy named Keith and his dad named Roddy. Ever since Keith was a little boy he had always liked fishing. So did his dad because his dad's dad had taught him to fish so it had more or less run in the family.

One Saturday, in the holidays, they towed their boat down to the pier and loaded it with fishing equipment and sailed away at dawn. The place they were aiming for was a group of islands called Anglers Dusk. They had heard some tales and myths of travellers' sightings of a monster that turned their boats and swam away under the surface. They didn't take any notice, but they had been warned.

After an hour of sailing, they reached their destination and by now it was bright and sunny. They had started fishing. Keith got a bite. He had hooked a fish. *Quite a big one by the bend of the rod*, Roddy thought. After say five minutes Keith was still there, struggling with this big fish, so Roddy came over and gave him a hand with it. But not even Roddy could get it in and he was stronger.

After a minute, the line went loose. They thought they had lost it and they were disappointed. Then they saw a shadow coming straight at them. It went all quiet. It flipped the boat right over and they've never been seen since.

Duncan Macrae (13)
Sgoil Nan Loch, Isle Of Lewis

FAMILY TREE

It was the school holidays. I was bored, so I decided to go down the library. When I got in the library I had a look for a book. I could hear someone calling me.

'Holly.'

I looked around and there was my best friend, Polly. She was in the family tree section. I had always thought family trees were boring. I sat down beside Polly and she told me to search out my family tree, so I did.

I eventually found my family tree. I was very surprised at how the book was so big. I started to look through it. At first I found it was quite boring because I didn't really know any of the names.

I began to look back to the *very* start of the book. I saw a very unusual name but it seemed to stick out. It was 'Charlie Pride'. Polly said he was an old country singer. I didn't believe her so I decided that I'd do some research.

I went on a library computer and began to research. I was very surprised to see that Charlie Pride was actually an old country singer, but I didn't know whether or not to believe that I could be related to him. I carried on researching about him. I couldn't see a way of getting in contact with him, which was sad. I went home and told my mum. She didn't believe me.

But I believe that I am related to someone famous!

Karen Mackenzie (13)
Sgoil Nan Loch, Isle Of Lewis

THIS TIME OF YEAR AGAIN!

Hi. I'm Dougal McCoy, I'm 11 years old. My mates call me Super Speed after my go-kart. It was the time of the kids' go-kart races last year and I came first! Now the time is here again for the race. All of my mates are taking part - Bob, Donald, Roy, Seth and this rich lad who has just moved from England. He lives in the massive house at the end of the road. I heard that he has a top of the range go-kart! OK, yes, I know it sounds like a good kart, but nothing can beat my 'Super Speed'. I just have to go to the garage, I know it's there somewhere.

It needs work, the race is in two days. There is Mum calling me in.
'Dougal!'
'OK, I'm up!'
'All ready for the race son?'
'Yes Dad, I'm all set.'

'Alright Bob, nice kart.'
Bing bong: 'Will all drivers please take their places!'
'OK Dougal, you can do this,' Dad said.
There is that rich lad. *Wow,* look at his kart!
5, 4, 3, 2, 1, *go! Wow, whoooo! Waw!* I'm 1st. Oh look, there is the posh lad! There he is taking off ahead of me. Oh no, there is the finish line!
'And 1st place goes to Razor Blade! And 2nd place to Super Speed!'
Nooo, I came second! I gave the posh boy a glare. 'Och well, there is always next year,' I said.

Jane Macleod (13)
Sgoil Nan Loch, Isle Of Lewis

A SHORT STORY COMING FROM... A DOG

I'm called Ellie and my life's a complete mess. I live in the horrible kennels, waiting to be re-homed, but nobody wants me because of my age.

I wake up to the sound of barking, again, although I didn't have a good sleep anyway. Well, who would? All I've got in my cage is a tiny little rag and a dusty food bowl which is never filled.

I just lay by my cage door, waiting to be free, then the person who walks me came at last. I am so excited to see him, although he isn't very nice at all.

I heard that the other dogs get to go on a fresh green field, but all I go on is an isolated area filled with concrete and there's not once piece of grass in sight. I try and run away, but I forget I'm on a lead, so I start choking and he smacks me and tells me to shut up.

Finally I get back and I am so happy to see my cage. People start looking at me, but in a really strange way and it isn't because I am so thin, it is because I am bleeding where my walker has been pulling at me.

They are putting their fingers through the bar and someone went to get the person who owns the place to come and take a look at me. Before I know it everyone is around me, even the vets. I feel really dizzy and then I am sick so the vets have to carry me out and I have to have an injection which puts me to sleep.

The next time I see daylight is the day after and I am lying on a big four-poster bed. I don't know where I am but I really did like it.

I decide to wander off and then I hear someone coming, so I try to run back to the bed. The person sees me and tells me to go down. She puts me in the kennels, but she is really nice because she gives me treats and lots of hugs. She comes to me every day. She also decorated my kennels.

Adelaide Stokes (12)
The Priory School, Shropshire

A Day In The Life Of An Abused Horse

My stable was so cold. My mane felt like it was turning into icicles. I hadn't eaten for days. My master was coming towards me. Oh no. She was carrying a saddle and bridle. As the short, plump, strict woman walked into my stable, I put my ears back. She dumped the saddle on me and tightened the girth until I couldn't breath. She yanked the bit into my mouth until the sides of my mouth bled, again.

She pulled me out of my stable harshly. She led me into a huge field with thick, sticky mud that came up to the top of my hooves. She heaved her heavy body onto my fragile back. She dug her heels into my scarred stomach, and the torture started.

We had been going for at least an hour. I was starting to get tired so I slowed down, but she kept whipping me harder, until at last I couldn't go any more. With one last crack of her demon whip, I collapsed and fell to the ground.

My master immediately got off me and dragged me back to my wretched stable. She whipped me again and said, 'That ought to show you.'

Finally she left me. My knees were bleeding. I was so thirsty but my water was green and gave off an awful smell. I was hungry but all the food I had was some old potato peelings. Finally I lay down on the hard concrete and dreaded what tomorrow would bring.

Lauren Walker (12)
The Priory School, Shropshire

THE HORROR PAINTING

This tale starts long ago when they believed in witches.

If you get scared easily, stop reading, for I am about to tell you the horrors that await greedy people!

This tale is about a young woman called Isabella Mackintosh who moved to London to make a fortune. She became an innkeeper but business was not good.

One night she found herself opening the front door to an old woman. When she asked the lady for the sum of one guinea, she found that the woman was no more than a beggar, so she said, 'Be gone, old beggar, and never return.'
The lady looked at the young woman. All she could see was greed, but she needed somewhere to stay, so she gave up her most beloved possession, a painting that her mother had given her, in exchange for a room.

That night the lady lay awake thinking. She decided to put a curse on the painting so whoever looked at it, misfortune would find them.

As she left the next morning, she said to Isabella, 'To stop it, give - don't take.'
Isabella thought that the old woman was disturbed in her mind and went to admire the painting, but soon after that she got word that her father was dead and after that she became very ill herself.

One night, a poor man came to her. She remembered the old lady's words and didn't charge him. Immediately she recovered and vowed never to be greedy again.

Laura Veecock (12)
The Priory School, Shropshire

CAT AND MOUSE

Kevin shivered. Appledown Terrace. It's where she lived, the witch! Would she see him? He had to go into her garden, his new ball was there and Mum would kill him if he didn't get it back.

He opened the creaky gate. Strange, her milk had been there since yesterday, no doubt to lure neighbourhood cats. Even so, Kevin had a bad feeling. He searched for his ball; there it was, caught between a prickly bush and a dandelion. He reached down to pick it up when a voice caught him off balance.
'You come here!'
Kevin stopped; he was bound to be turned into a frog or something.
The witch shouted again, 'You,' but this time it was softer, more gentle.
He slowly turned, but to his amazement there was a beautiful young woman.
She spoke again, 'Come in and have a drink. I don't bite you know.'
Kevin hesitated, then picking up his ball he went to the door. 'I though you were a witc . . . I mean, an old woman,' he spluttered, trying to correct himself.
'Where did you get that idea?' she asked, as if angel was her middle name.

She wound her arm around him and led him inside, picking up the milk bottles as she went. A smile crept from her face, no longer beautiful, she had turned into a wrinkly old woman with cat-like features. Licking her lips she whispered into his ear, 'Would you like some milk?'
The door slammed behind her.

Helen Alexander (14)
The Priory School, Shropshire

THE FRIGHTENING FOREST

The wind roared and the branches thrashed in the woods. A child ran through the forest and into the night. She jumped as a bolt of lightning destroyed the tree behind her. A laugh that sounded more like a scream than a laugh rang through the trees. Sandy, for that was this wretched girl's name, turned around wondering what being could possibly possess such an inhuman laugh. The laugh echoed once more through the woods. It rattled in her ears and made her legs turn to jelly. Despite her fear she could not stop herself from following the laughter, walking towards her doom.

Sandy crept towards the clearing. She crawled closer. She saw a huge bonfire and the most horrifying group of people that she had ever seen. There was a small, slimy monster whose eyes were like balls of fire. A worm-like creature slithered through the undergrowth; it had a mouth full of teeth that were covered in a sticky coat of saliva. But worst of all was a woman that would make even the most deformed women bless their luck that they did not look like her. Her hair hung down over her shoulders like seaweed and her skin looked like she had torn it off and sewn it back on many times.

These three creatures would be the last living things Sandy ever saw. Paralysed with fear, she could only sit and wait for them to pounce.

That night a scream echoed through the woods.

Holly Edwards (12)
The Priory School, Shropshire

LIVE OFF THE STAGE

They close the curtains on my command. I can't reach them. I don't have the strength for that anymore.

It's the little things I miss the most. Everyone says that. What I wouldn't give to have the old times back. Walking, running - even going to the bathroom unaided would be a blessing.

The chaplain came to bless me yesterday. That's a signal. The end is near. I wish for the ending every moment - the final curtain call. Looking back, I wouldn't even make it to the publishers. I'd be the dusty old script on the top shelf - no fans. No followers. Unrecognisable from the shiny new masterpieces in the shops.

I'm unrecognisable now. Thin face, sagging features, balding dome. Who wants to end up like this? Is this all my life is worth to them - a narrow grey bed and a chamber pot? Bald, bedridden, belittled. A shadow of my former self. No visitors.

No visitors. Who'd come? Looking in the mirror doesn't scare me anymore, but looking at me terrifies anyone who isn't used to it. I'm so . . . *different*. One glance and they start to worry. I shall eat them alive. One glimpse and they'll see what could be. What indefinitely *will* be. They can't face the facts.

The nurse closes my curtains. She does it because I ask her, but who'd peek?

It's not the cancer. I am.

Caroline James (15)
The Priory School, Shropshire

LOVE

The wind howled piercingly against the windows as she sat, motionless. It wouldn't be long now.

Her hands shook as she fumbled her knitting needles, dropping stitches, but not noticing. Her mind was elsewhere, vacant, somewhere where everything was good and the people you loved never hurt you. A surreal place.

She jolted in panic as she heard a tap at the door and stiffened, thinking for a moment that she had miscalculated the time. But it was just a leaf, whipped up by the screaming wind and unseen in the growing gloom. He would be back soon, as he always was. When he ran out of money.

It was odd, the way love and pain were so close together. How one always came closely entwisted in the other, as tangled as a briar bush, complete with thorns and hopeless to separate. How something so beautiful and something so wretched could be bound together to harmonise, to make sense. Almost.

Pain, in some ways, is like love. It is sweet, sweet agony, and it is a sacrifice. Pain is sacrifice, and to love, one must sacrifice. It makes perfect sense, doesn't it? Maybe they are one and the same thing. Maybe they are both different in ways of sacrifice, undertaking suffering for someone. In a way you could say that pain is a form of love. Yes. That's right. Pain is a sort of love.

She jumped again as the door crashed open, this time for real. Her husband was home.

Siobhan Hinton (14)
The Priory School, Shropshire

THE DAY I SAW THE LOCH NESS MONSTER...

It all started when I went on holiday with my family up to Scotland. I kept asking whether we could go abroad but my parents were set on the idea. My younger brother, Luke, wanted to go down to Loch Ness to see if he could spot the legendary Loch Ness monster and that's where I saw it.

'Are we nearly there yet?' shouted Luke from the back seat for the millionth time.
'Nearly,' sighed Mum heavily.
I could tell by her voice that she wasn't as keen on the idea of having a holiday up in Scotland.

The sky was turning an ugly grey and soon enough rain started to pour. I pressed my face up against the window, wishing I was in Florida, when my dad interrupted my thoughts.
'We're here!' he announced in an annoyingly cheery voice.
I jumped down from the car and looked up at the castle we had arranged to be staying in. It looked more like a prison than anything else. High, grey stone walls with few windows. I dragged my feet up the gravel path and started to write 'Wish I wasn't here' with my foot. I quickly scrubbed it out as the big oak door opened and out came a small, weird-looking man.
'Good afternoon!' he said, a big toothy grin spreading over his face.
'Hi,' I muttered. Luckily, Mum had just come that second to save me from the awkward conversation.
'Hello, I'm Mrs Bennet, can we come in?' Mum asked.
'Of course,' smiled the man, and with that me and my family stumbled in.
'Lovely place you got 'ere!' shouted Dad embarrassingly.
'Thanks,' mumbled the man under his breath. 'May I suggest you leave your bags here and visit the Loch?' asked the man, his ugly smile appearing again on his face.
'Uhhh . . . yeah!' shrugged Mum and with that we trudged back to our car and drove to Loch Ness.

The sky was getting really grey by that time but at least it wasn't raining. While my dad was busy telling off Luke and Mum was staring at this bird, I decided to go for a walk. I must admit that it was very peaceful and calm. I then found myself staring into the Loch. I couldn't make out what it was, it was black, maybe very dark green, however, it started swimming towards me. I took a step forward to get a better look. 'Wow,' I breathed. 'I've seen the monster!' It was beautiful, shimmering in the light. It was getting closer and closer, almost just five foot away from me. I stretched my arm out to touch the magnificent gentle creature.

'Oi! Come on, we're going now!' shouted Luke.
I nearly jumped out of my skin. The monster vanished with a splash. Gone, forever! I was just glad I had been lucky enough to see it!

Mia Tivey (12)
The Priory School, Shropshire

A Day In The Life Of A Great White Shark!

9.01: Aah! Ouh! Oh hi . . . I'm Sharky the great white shark. Why do ya have to wake me up? There's no problem sleeping in my *new* coral bed, which is so *soooo* comfy. Actually it's a good idea you woke me. Looking at my schedule, it looks like it's breakfast which today is . . . Coco Pops! Yipee I just love 'em!

10.15: Finished those lovely Coco Pops. Now I think I'll do a bit of gardening in my garden of fish and coral. My garden is just the *best* out of all my friends' (theirs are horrible, they don't look after them at all). Anyway if they don't want to look after them like I do then that's alright. Just a bit more coral there and I think I've done it! Yes, that's it!

11.49: What shall I do next? Oh yes, I'll just go over to my schedule which has me swimming around the Canary Islands. This time I'm going to absolutely thrash my time to bits. Yesterday it took me eight long hours, but today, hopefully, I'll beat it. Yesterday I got geared up for the next one. But first my schedule says lunch at 12.00, so it is beans on toast (nice).

Finished that so I'll see you later at about 7.30. Bye!

7.29 and 38.58 seconds: Have . . . have . . . I've done it! Oh yes! What a record! I even stopped off at my mate's house to ha . . . v . . . e . . . a . . . b . . . e . . . e . . . r. *Zzzz.*

Eloise Jackson (11)
The Priory School, Shropshire

SECRET OF THE DARKNESS

Have you ever been alone? All alone? Stood there, watching, waiting ...?

Many years ago, on the deserted, windswept hills of Dartmoor, a small boy stood alone. Shrouded with mist, the moon illuminated his pale face. He shivered as his thin shirt blew around in the chilling wind. Slowly, he dug his bony, shaking hands into the pockets of his worn trousers and glanced anxiously around.

Nobody knew who he was and nobody knew why he stood there, except one ...

An eerie silence filled the night air as dark clouds skimmed across the sky. The small boy turned, glancing fearfully around him, as if being watched by someone or something ...

A loud, mournful howl ripped suddenly through the still night air. The boy jumped, his eyes wide with fear. The wind in the trees whispered, as if telling a secret; a secret to the dark night ...

Slowly it rose and in the darkness of its lair it waited ...

Rachel Benson (12)
The Priory School, Shropshire

A Day In The Life Of A ... Paramedic

7.00am
The early morning staff are ready to rock 'n' roll! It's a good job to be honest, because it's the International Football Club final today, so there are bound to be a few punch-ups here and there! It looks as if it's going to be a jam-packed shift! I can just see it now, the footie maniacs bringing some of their 'disagreements' into the Accident & Emergency waiting room!

7.10am
Now we're ready for some real action! There's an incoming call and here we go; it's a motorway pile-up. Something like this was expected today! We've just got here and it seems pretty awful to me! There are about eight to ten cars involved as well as a truck. You guessed it, they are *all* footie fans except the truck driver who was a foreigner!

Eleven of the men came out without even a scratch on them and the other five were taken to hospital for a check-up, but everyone was at the ground in time for kick-off. Thank God!

8.45am
Wow! There were no calls for over an hour and a half (bargain)! We've had a call from a telephone box reporting a hit 'n' run. Most of the calls we receive from phone boxes are usually kids messing about and I don't see why this one would be an exception, but by law we have to attend every call even if we have our suspicions.

9.05am
We're back at the hospital now. It's time for a break in twenty-five minutes and our shift ends at half-past twelve. The football match won't finish until about six, half-six, so our crew will be out of the way for major crashes or riots!

9.30am
Time for a tea break! If we get a call during the break we have to leave everything and attend as soon as possible. It has been a hard day so far, but it might not seem like it to you. To get a real taster of the job you would have to do it!

11.55am
Oh! We've just received a last minute call to a house on the corner of this road. Now we are in the house and the stupid bloke has called us out 'cause he has a cramp in his leg! All he had to do was put pressure and walk about on it. *Pathetic!*

Lisa Patel
The Streetly School, West Midlands

BEOWULF V GRENDEL'S MOTHER

It was the middle of the night. Beowulf, Lentric and I were sleeping when all of a sudden I heard a rustling noise. I peeped open my eyes, surprised to see two servants waking Beowulf up.

They were taking him to Hrothgar (who was the king of Herot) as he had news of a terrible events that had happened during the night - Grendel's mother had come to avenge her son. She grabbed the nearest Geat who just happened to be a friend of mine. Aschere was his name, she grabbed him and carried him off under her arm. If I had been awake I probably would have been able to prevent this terrible crime.

Beowulf then decided, as ever, he would go and seek out Grendel's mother and kill her.

So we all set off on a great journey. We sliced through mist and battled past weeds until we reached the sea wolf's lair.

Beowulf continued on - he wanted to do this on his own so we held back. Grendel's mother suddenly appeared out of the lair, red-eyed and roaring. She grabbed him and swept him deep down into an underwater chamber.

Great Beowulf with his sword tried to slash Grendel's mother's head but it just bounced off as she was protected by a magic spell.

Grendel's mother then pulled Beowulf's head back and lunged towards him with a dagger. It went into his chest but he too was protected, not by a magic spell, but just by the fine chainmail I made for him.

Beowulf lunged towards her. The blade went through her neck in one clean sweep, blood splattered everywhere. We could see the lake turning red, bubbling blood overflowing. The King and his men left, thinking Beowulf was dead.

Beowulf stood and stared at the beheaded monster. As he did so, the sword which had been touched by poisoned blood, shrivelled away in his hands, so he was left with a handle.

Beowulf's eyes then moved to a cave in the corner. He went to inspect, he got a shock. Grendel's body lay lifeless over in the corner. With his own sword he slashed off Grendel's head. He would take this as a trophy of his braveness.

When he did appear at the surface, we all cheered. He had done it, he had defeated the beasts. We had two brilliant banquets with an all you can eat buffet!

Beowulf deserved this party for his wonderful, fantastic victory.

Harriet Aldam (12)
Wakefield Girls' High School, West Yorkshire

BEOWULF V GRENDEL'S MOTHER

Now, I remember the time many years back when Beowulf killed Grendel's mother. We were all relaxing after the terrifying trauma with Grendel when the King's messenger appeared and told us we had to get back to Heorot immediately as the King had an urgent message. We were all puzzled by this, but set off to Heorot straight away.

When we all arrived, we were hustled into the great hall. The King told us that last night Grendel's mother had torn down Grendel's arm from the gable and had stormed in and grabbed one of the King's men, Aschere. We were all horrified at this statement. How could it be? We thought we'd finished the monster business once and for all. Beowulf exclaimed that we should go and find Grendel's mother as we should not be defeated just like that, when their mate Aschere was at stake.

So it was settled, the next day we set off to follow Grendel's mother's tracks. We travelled through great cities and over magnificent countryside with breathtaking views. Finally we came to a dark, misty lake on the edge of the forest. We could see a lonesome figure rising from the lake. Beowulf told us to get back. The figure hurled itself up out of the lake. It was Grendel's mother! She grabbed hold of Beowulf by the neck and threw him down under the water with her into a secret underwater cave.

We waited ages, the King and most of his men left after losing hope. All we could see was a sea of red blood skimming the water. The people that were left of us were all awfully scared of what could have happened to Beowulf. We waited for nine hours, when at last Beowulf came to the surface of the water, holding the handle of a golden sword and the head of Grendel. We all had a joyful feeling of relief inside us.

Beowulf told us that he tried killing Grendel's mother with his own sword, but she had a curse on her so she could only be killed by a magic sword. He found the sword and hacked her to death. Her own blood melted the blade of the sword.

The King was tremendously overwhelmed when he found out and invited us all to the great hall for a feast. We laughed and ate to our heart's content and drank masses of ale. There was also a huge cake iced with 'Thank you Beowulf'. The party went on till 2am, then we all just dropped to the floor.

Lucy Alliott (12)
Wakefield Girls' High School, West Yorkshire

THE SILVER LADY

It was Hallowe'en at Ackworth School. The large stone building stood alone surrounded by acres of land. The walls had fragrant roses and ivy climbing up them. The trees were dancing in the cool, calm, crisp breeze. Some of the window ledges were freshly painted and the smell still lingered around. The others were thick with dust. Anyone who washed those windows would have a nose and throat clogged with it.

In the whole building only one light was on. In the room were two girls. One girl had a soft complexion, cheeks as red as roses, full lips, golden hair as soft as silk and deep blue eyes like pools of enchantment. She was sat listening to her friend in her Winnie the Pooh pyjamas. The girl's name was Jenny.

Jade (her friend) had pale cheeks, unlike Jenny. She also had deep chestnut eyes, crimson lips and auburn hair. She also had her pyjamas on, but these ones had Little Miss Naughty on them.

The room was pleasant and cosy, it smelt of winter spices. It was based around the colours green and blue. The springy beds were still tidily made, they had bluebell patterns on the duvets. On some new shelves were some ornamental glass bluebells. By now Jade had finished talking.

'My turn!' said Jenny. 'Right, this horror story is set in this school. Many, many years ago, people had to go and ring the bell in the clock tower. The lady who did it when this story is set was known as the 'silver lady'. She was called this because she always wore silver or grey silk and lace. She had an ice-white face, long blonde, silky hair, cold blue eyes and thin lips. She never wore make-up.

One night, (on Hallowe'en in fact) the silver lady walked along the dark wooden floor. Her shoes made a clicking sound as she carried her dimly lit candle. Very slowly she crept up the long ladder to the top of the clock tower. Inside was very dark, the candle did not let off much light.

It was midnight and the silver lady, also known as Angela, was being very careful. She rang the bell twelve times. As she was carefully walking back to the ladder she saw a tiny white mouse. It startled her so much she jumped back in amazement. When she did this she caught the bell, pulled it an extra time by mistake, then fell down the centre of the clock tower to her death.'

'Scary. It's not true is it?' asked Jade.
'Of course not!'
Just then they heard the clicking shoes outside. The girls jumped.
'What are we so scared for? It's only Mrs Smith checking we're asleep but she won't notice our light because I put my dressing gown at the bottom of the door!'
'I'm tired. What time is it?'
'I don't know, let's listen for the clock tower to chime. Here it comes: 1, 2, 3, 4, 5, 6, 7, 8, 9, 10, 11, 12. Night-night Jenny.'
Dong!

Alice Castle (11)
Wakefield Girls' High School, West Yorkshire

Silence

I felt emptiness had taken over the whole world. Nothing seemed alive, nothing made a noise and nothing had a smell. The whole world was dead. The long, yellowy grass was brittle, it obviously hadn't rained in weeks. The colossal dark shadows made sunlight blinding. Immensely long, countrified storage houses stretched across the land, there were no windows or doors on these storage houses, just pointed roofs. They were so basic and ordinary that they were almost indescribable.

Shadows appeared everywhere you walked like ghosts haunting you as soon as you're born. Bare treetops peeped over the buildings as if they were trying to see what was happening. Except there wasn't anything happening, everything was still, soundless but deadly!

I saw a winding path with a white outline. As I stared at it a question jumped to my mind, *why would anyone want to walk down it leading to a deserted spine-chilling area?*

And that's when I saw him . . .

Samantha Antwis (12)
Wakefield Girls' High School, West Yorkshire

THE WONDERFUL HOUSE

I turned the corner and stood in amazement, looking around at the garden which was filled with flowers. The Victorian house had gigantic patio doors leading out to the garden and a greenhouse with juicy red tomatoes and appetising green grapes growing in it.

I heard something move quickly behind me. It gave me a fright. I turned around and realised that it was only a frog, but it was in a fabulous pond which was sparkling and twinkling because the bright sun was shining on it.

I went to look at all of the flowers, they were fantastic. They were all the colours that you could imagine. I bent down to smell the ruby-red roses and the violet carnations, they smelt so lovely, just like a lady putting on her perfume ready for a night out.

I crept over to the house and peered into the hall to make sure nobody was in there. I looked around, there was a gold staircase and a sofa with a silk throw on it. I looked through the patio doors into the lounge. It had a widescreen TV and another two of those posh sofas.

I walked over to the greenhouse and my mouth was watering just looking at the lush tomatoes and grapes. I saw an apple tree behind the greenhouse. I was just about to pick an apple and that's when I saw him . . .

Jessica Barrell (11)
Wakefield Girls' High School, West Yorkshire

GRENDEL'S MOTHER

'Gather round children, come up close so you can hear me. I'm becoming a little rusty in my old age. I'm about to tell you all the story of Grendel's manipulative mother.

She was just like him in some respects. Anyway, you may remember the brave, warrior-hero Beowulf, who slaughtered Grendel at an early age and sacrificed his own troop Leofric. Yet again, he is our hero.

Well, it all started when two humble servants woke Beowulf from his dream-filled sleep and frog-marched him to Hrothgar's (the King of Heorot) candlelit chamber. Hrothgar informed Beowulf that Grendel's mother had barged into the great hall and seized a man nearby. As fate would have it, he just happened to be the King's best friend, Aeschere. It was clear that this was revenge for her son.

However, Beowulf had other ideas for the Sea-wolf and he promised Hrothgar that he would kill her and return victorious. He led us away and over the misty moors, at the bottom of the lake where her underground lair remained. Beowulf also promised that wherever she wandered, he would closely follow.

At nightfall, he took his finest stallion and was accompanied to the lake by the King, the Geats and some Danes. When they arrived, the lake was filled with blood and Grendel's mother immediately spotted us and she pulled him into a great vaulted chamber, which was untouched by water. Beowulf decided it was time to defend himself, so he hit her hard across the forehead, but it didn't harm her in the slightest bit.

He threw the sword away and began to grapple with her. He knocked her down, but she tripped him up and drew a dagger to his heart. However, his chainmail saved him. He jumped up and saw a magic sword made by superior giants, lying in the corner. He picked it up and swung it at her and it soared through her neck and smashed her vertebrae. The monster died at his feet.

Next door, he found Grendel and slashed off his head, however, his venom melted the sword up to its hilt! (But he took them as trophies anyway.) When he swam back up to the surface he was greeted by me and his fellow companions, who escorted him back to the royal banquet, where they feasted.'

Joanne Morris (12)
Wakefield Girls' High School, West Yorkshire

BEOWULF V GRENDEL'S MUM

When I was a young boy at the plucky age of 17, I was asked to go to Heorot with the almighty Beowulf. The legendary King Hrothgar, had asked him to come because he wanted to try to kill a monster called Grendel, who was terrorising the great hall of his palace. Beowulf and I accepted at once and we began our ride the next day.

The journey to Heorot was long and tiring. When we got there it was already dark, mysterious and very eerie. We waited in the great hall for Grendel. We waited and waited until finally we heard the disgusting gurgling and slurping of the sickening monster. I tell you now, it made my stomach churn. The monster ambled into the hall. He tried to grab the nearest thing to him, which actually happened to be me, but luckily he just knocked me out the way. Instead, he seized Leofric, one of Beowulf's soldiers and devoured him, armour and all. Subsequently, Beowulf avenged Leofric's death by killing Grendel, severing Grendel's arm with his bare hands. He hung the appendage on the gable as a trophy of his victory. That memory will stick with me forever.

Beowulf didn't know what would follow. Grendel's mother would take vengeance by attacking the great hall and snatching her dead son's limb. She had to be stopped! She had already killed the King's best comrade, Aeschere. So the King, a troop of Danes, Beowulf and a few of his Geat companions set off to the sea wolf's lair. They followed the putrid stench and her footprints.

The sea wolf's lair was at the bottom of a cold, dark, life-threatening lake. Just looking at it scared me. Suddenly, Grendel's mother rose out of the water and grabbed a startled Beowulf and dragged him to the bottom of the lake. The King waited for nine hours and when Beowulf didn't return, the King assumed them dead and returned to the palace to mourn.

Beowulf struggled and escaped her grasp. He tried to stab her with his sword, but she had been protected by a magic spell. She loomed in on him and jabbed at his muscular torso, with a razor-sharp dagger, but his robust chainmail rescued him. In this confusion, he noticed a colossal double-sided sword. So, with the strength of a thousand men, Beowulf picked up the sword. It was as big as the giants who had made it. He pounded her about the head again and again, ending her life forever and ever.

He caught sight of Grendel slumped in the corner, drained of his life's blood. He decided to take what was rightfully his and slashed off Grendel's head with one clean sweep.

He was incredibly proud of his souvenirs, Grendel's head and the enchanted sword. He was devastated when the sword melted away in his hands. Nevertheless, the jewelled hilt remained intact. Exhausted, Beowulf started to leave the lair to tell the fantastic news to the King. He found out later, that the sea-solf's blood had melted the sword.

Helen Palfrey (12)
Wakefield Girls' High School, West Yorkshire

The Scrapyard

I had to escape. I couldn't let them find me. Then I saw the scrapyard. It was the perfect place to hide in. In I ran, searching for anywhere big enough to hide a boy of my age, but all I could see was pile upon pile of crushed and battered cars, each a different shade of rusting metal. There were skips and bottle banks, cranes and bulldozers, and endless heaps of rubbish.

I crept into a pile of tyres, they were pitch-black and were caked in a thick layer of dry and flaking mud. I couldn't stand it. I ran further into the jungle of junk. Here the cranes towered over me as if I had shrunk and the further into the place I went, the harder the ground felt beneath my feet.

The centre of the scrapyard was full of old parts from cars, aged old bikes, toys that small children had grown out of, moth-eaten mattresses, and smashed china ornaments.

I walked between two newly painted trucks and came out on the edge of the scrapyard. I decided if I went out the police might find me, so I re-entered the safety of the fetid tip.

On my way back in I found a little white caravan where I expected the watchman to live and then something stirred. I dived into a clump of bushes and that's when I saw him . . .

Kate Elizabeth Hulley (12)
Wakefield Girls' High School, West Yorkshire

BUILDING SITE

I climbed over the gate, ignoring the danger sign. The gate shuddered and clanged for a second before it was still and silent. Cranes stood high up in the air, JCBs moving from one place to another, cement mixers whizzing around making sure there were no lumps. I tiptoed a little further to see a herd of builders stacking bricks on top of each other. Skips and skipfulls of bricks, metals, steel, paper and sandwich wrappers. I peered a little further, I felt a spider's cobweb fall onto my head. I peered into a small, clear jar, there were squished spiders, dead ants and at the side of the jar, a dead bird. I heard a ringing concussion from behind the skip, I took a glimpse around . . . and that's when I saw him!

Reena Patel (12)
Wakefield Girls' High School, West Yorkshire

BEOWULF V GRENDEL'S MOTHER

It was late one night in Herot in 1445, when the King called on me.
'Quick, gather up some men and bring Beowulf to me, I have a task for him,' the King, Horothgar ordered.
As quick as a flash, I found myself travelling to the mysterious cave of Grendel's mother.

When we finally arrived, all was still for a while. Suddenly a huge roar and an arm came out of the lake Frospa and hauled Beowulf into the lake. He said he was taken to a great vaulted chamber, a hell underwater, but it was totally untouched by water. What we (well, definitely I) hadn't noticed was that some Geats had been taken down too by the seawolf - Grendel's mother.

No matter how much they tried to kill her, it was no use. She was protected by magic spells. Beowulf tried hand-to-hand combat. Grendel's mother stabbed at Beowulf, but his chainmail was strong - I had made it. Beowulf said that he saw a huge magic sword laying in the corner of the chamber. He got himself free, picked up the sword and slaughtered the gruesome beast.

Meanwhile, above the lake, we were all waiting in anticipation. We had waited for nine, long, gruelling hours. We saw blood rising from the lake, it was either Grendel's or Beowulf's. Everyone's heart sank, expecting the worst. At this moment, the King and his men left. After about 30 minutes the gallant Beowulf rose from the stained lake, clutching the distorted head of Grendel's mother and we all rejoiced.

When we got back to Herot and the King knew, we all *partied!* I bet you never knew how much of a party animal I used to be. There were rows upon rows of food, reaching for miles. There were huge plates of pork, chicken and lamb. Also sausage rolls and humungous dishes of jelly and fruit. But the pièce de résistance was the cake. It was huge, with chocolate and plain cake, decorated with swirls of vanilla, strawberry and mint icing. It was certainly a night to remember!

Vicky Peacock (12)
Wakefield Girls' High School, West Yorkshire

HIM!

As I went to retrieve my new cricket ball from our new next-door neighbours' garden, I felt uneasy. Uneasy because they might not approve of me invading their property or that their children were bullies and were jeering at me that very second, like the last inhumane children used to. But I also noticed their garden was much more picturesque than ours, everything was so neat and colourful.

A small path surrounded a small pond which contained all sorts of tropical water plants and frisky fish. To the left of the path were probably thirty different kinds of flowers, from red roses to yellow daffodils, to things I don't know the names of. They ranged from minuscule pansies to gigantic sunflowers. The vibrant colours were so strong they gave off their own light, literally. Much of the greenery was bedded in black and white pebbles.

I carefully and silently trod along the grey path, but to get to the house you had to cross several circular stepping stones. I leapt from one to the other, avoiding trampling their obviously freshly mowed lawn. The sweet smell of lavender tickled my nose, which caused me to trip. Luckily, I didn't attract any attention.

The front door was left ajar just like one of their windows. Hesitantly, I stepped in, calling their names, but no response followed. I presumed they weren't home. Their porch was rather dull, dark and dreary compared to the garden, it was completely bare.

I hopped back outside again to see a glass greenhouse. At the front tomatoes were ripening. Many minute bushes, in all shades of green, were enclosing a section of the greenhouse. In front of the bushes, right next to me, stood a large green rain collector. I wondered if my ball could be inside it, so I peered down to the bottom and that's when I saw him . . .

Ileena Pramanik (12)
Wakefield Girls' High School, West Yorkshire

WGHS Horror

I clutched the crooked banister and swung open the heavy door.
'Boo!' screeched Nicky from behind me.
'You scared me! What are you doing here?' I questioned her and sat down on the ugly brown desk.
'Remember, we're all meeting up to check out the mysterious noises and what they are,' she replied with quivering lips.
'Where's Harriet?' I asked, tearing a piece of paper out of my rough book.
'I'm here,' she giggled and drew back the long red curtains.
'How long have you been there?' I panted.
'I came just before Julie,' a broad smile appeared on Harriet's face.

We squeezed out of the door and headed for the room, the one and only room which always had the sound of someone weeping inside. I barged through the brightly coloured door and started to search through the wooden drawers.
'Look at this,' yelled Nicky in surprise.
Harriet waddled over like a duck, to the drawer that Nicky was tightly holding. I also targeted the drawer. Inside the drawer there was an unpleasant pair of small black shoes.
'Why do you find that important? Shoes don't make noises.' I yelled, squeezing my fists together.
'You're not very observant are you Julie, look, look inside the shoe,' Nicky wailed.

I sighed and plodded over to the drawer and inside there was a small, brown bag which carried lots of fake money in. I shook the bag and tipped out all of the silver coins and examined them one by one and I quietly stepped outside and ran down the long, dark corridor, but they didn't follow me so I continued to tremble, watching the sides as I sped past. My shoes were brushing against the brown floor. I was so scared that something or someone would jump out on me as I was all alone in this huge school. Visions of horrible monsters raced in circles around my head. *Should I go back?* I thought to myself.

'I need to file my nails.'
I turned around and realised that Harriet wasn't far away. Phew. I took a deep breath and charged down to Harriet and Nicky.
'Look, let's face it Julie, the noise is definitely in the English block,' Nicky howled, trying to act all cool and stylish.
I stomped along the hall. The moon kept winking at me through the murky windows.
'Where are you going Julie?' Harriet called from the side.
'Up to room 24,' I replied. By this time I was really angry, I had to figure out this mystery before it was too late!

As I dashed up the twisting staircase I heard a strange noise which was ringing in my ear, like a bleeping watch. I gritted my sensitive teeth, turned the handle of the staffroom door and plunged onto the floor. It was nothing, it was all me hearing things.

Clocks were ticking. I only had one hour until dawn and I was feeling very sleepy, but I carried on up the stairs. I grasped the shiny handle and pushed open the door to room 24. It looked like a bomb had just hit it. There were books scattered on the floor, cupboard doors swaying with the fresh breeze, curtains flapping, desks creaking and the computer was flashing.

I had searched through every drawer but one. I ripped out the drawer, trembling with fear and laying there, was a rotten skull. I knelt down and felt it, but it just crumbled away in my hands.

Sarah Smith (11)
Wakefield Girls' High School, West Yorkshire

THE CLUTTERED SCRAPYARD

One summer Sunday evening I crept through the rusted mesh fence of the scrapyard. The air was warm and dusty and smelt strongly of oil from the wrecked cars heaped all around. The two high, red cranes towered over me like menacing giants. The wind whistled with a high-pitched screech as it blew between the struts in the crane and made the loose strips of metal bang and crash. The low, soft sun made the shiny metal gleam and made dark, long shadows all around me. The dusty and dirty ground had small pieces of metal scattered everywhere like leaves that had fallen off the trees in autumn.

Suddenly behind me was a loud crashing of metal. As I spun round I looked more closely and saw a black, dirty cat creeping into the back of a rusty, old, doorless van. I nervously followed it. That's when I saw him . . .

Danielle Saunders (12)
Wakefield Girls' High School, West Yorkshire

LEGEND OF THE LABYRINTH

At last I was thrust into the dark labyrinth. There was a big noise as the door slammed behind me. Blinded by the light, I suddenly became aware of the stale air and the uninviting walls, waiting for me to fall into their enraged clasp.

As I walked on, leaving my trail of string behind me, I smelt fragmenting bodies of rats and what looked like humans. Anger flushed through me. To think that for many years my fellow people, my own flesh and blood had been slain in this living hell. I walked on, hearing the sound of dripping water. It seemed like an age of going back and forth to get through the passages, until there was a soft, distant scuttle of hooves, a distant roar of what had to be the Minotaur.

Seeing the beast was a sickly half-man, half-bull with blood dripping everywhere and the stains around its mouth, brought the taste of fear and anger into my mouth. I grabbed a stalagmite and used it as a sword, jabbing it here and there. My own body by now was a sorry sight. After the rush of fear I was butted against the unforgiving walls but then there was my chance to kill, to end, to thrust my rock through the beast.

I woke up seeing the sky, a seagull and people. I came home in a ship with white sails, docking into the port with a hero's welcome.

Beth Langley (11)
Ysgol Uwchradd Tregaron, Ceredigion

THE BOY WHO GOT LEFT BEHIND

Dear Diary,
My heart is filled with sadness, because today the Pied Piper took his pipe and blew it hard and all us children followed.

We all ran after him and skipped after him merrily. He led us to a beautiful land by the town. Waters gushed and marvellous fruit trees grew, flowers of all colours, shapes and sizes grew. Ah, it was a beautiful land. We followed him to near a mountainside. He led us through a door in the mountainside.

But I, I was too slow, I blame my lameness for that. I could not follow quickly enough and it is my sorrow that the door shut and I was left alone. The sound of the music vanished from his pipe. I had no choice but to sadly go back down the hill, back to Hamelin, without the company of my fellow playmates.

I feel sad, destroyed and weak. All my playmates and friends are gone. I really feel as if I cannot carry on. I am lonely now, writing this with all my friends gone, nobody to laugh and play with. I am alone also as all the townspeople have gone to look for the Pied Piper. I did not want to go, I just wanted to write this. I doubt if they will find him. The door would probably need to be opened by a magic pipe. I wish my friends would come back, if only they would, I have no one here, please come back, if only . . .

Rachel Burrowes (11)
Ysgol Uwchradd Tregaron, Ceredigion